Eclipse

Also by David Lehner

Bright Day
Unwelcome Light

ECLIPSE

~

a novel by

David Lehner

FITHIAN PRESS, MCKINLEYVILLE, CALIFORNIA, 2012

Copyright © 2012 by David Lehner
All rights reserved
Printed in the United States of America

The interior design and the cover design of this book are intended for and limited to the publisher's first print edition of the book and related marketing display purposes. All other use of those designs without the publisher's permission is prohibited.

Published by Fithian Press
A division of Daniel and Daniel, Publishers, Inc.
Post Office Box 2790
McKinleyville, CA 95519
www.danielpublishing.com

Distributed by SCB Distributors (800) 729-6423

LIBRARY OF CONGRESS CATALOGING-IN-PUBLICATION DATA
Lehner, David, (date)
Eclipse : a novel / by David Lehner.
   p. cm.
ISBN 978-1-56474-529-3 (pbk. : alk. paper)
I. Title.
PS3562.E4395E27 2012
813'.54—dc23
                   2012014589

*"Pretend I'm dead
and say something nice."*

—*Petronius,* Satyricon

Eclipse

~ Chapter One

"BUT SEE HERE," the young man said, "what about beauty? What about eloquence and the love of language? What do you think brought people to the study of poetry in the first place?"

"May I respond to that?" a small, gray, unkempt woman asked from the edge of the podium. "It is a remark of charming naiveté. If the young gentleman will kindly refer to his program he will see that we are not here to discuss eloquence or beauty. We are, rather, engaged in a quite specific subcategory of literary investigation, that is, the negotiation of textual desire in a context where truth and identity have become fragmented and problematized. A context without comforting universals where truth has become situational and therefore where sexual otherness overwrites the desire for semantic closure, or even approximation. This is the point Professor Quinn was making, and making quite well, I think, about vulvamorphia, the wrapping or embracing of semantic sites—a fluid system of relationships—and I emphasize "system" here—which perpetually erodes the dominant order through the wave forms of feminine libidinal energy. This makes desire, obviously, a political issue, and the text itself inherently political."

"Politics!" the young man shouted. "Politics! What do you know about politics? Nothing, I should guess. Why don't you stick to what you do know, or should know, which is literature? Why do you always have to take one thing and turn it into something else? Poetry isn't about politics, it isn't about your sex organs."

Another, still older professor shrugged his shoulders. "Young man, if we did what you say, who would come to our lectures? We can't make a living without our students. They call they shots. And, after all, most people just are interested in sex. It's what they want. So of course if you want to survive, it's what you have to give them."

"But I still must insist," the gray-haired old woman said, "that desire itself is inherently political, and, since that is the case...."

I could see that the debate would be likely to drag on interminably. I had no interest in hearing it to its end and left the auditorium as unobtrusively as possible. Once in the lobby, I noticed a group of students I had taken some classes with. I wouldn't normally have spoken to them, but one of them spotted me and waved me over. "What have you heard?" he asked me. "Anything good?"

"Nothing really. How about you?"

"We've just been to 'The Anus as Signifier.' It was tremendously brilliant. Really ground-breaking."

"Who? What?"

"Professor Kerne, of the Institute. I'll tell you, you really missed something."

"Oh."

"What are you attending next session?"

"I don't know. What do you suggest?"

"Try 'Inter(dis)course: Embedded Letters and Sexual Transgression in the Early English Novel.' And don't forget Susan's paper this afternoon on translation and transvestism. You'll be there, won't you?"

Susan, who was standing next to him and whom I vaguely knew, blushed with pride.

"Oh, yes," I said, "of course."

I left this group as quickly as possible and walked over to the cash bar sponsored by the Marxist Literary Group and bought an outrageously overpriced gin and tonic. After a while, people started to filter out of the main auditorium. There would be about twenty minutes before the next session began. I spread my program out on the bar and tried to figure out where I would go. "Critical Castration:" I read, "Pornography and Pop Culture in the Age of (dis)memberment." Somehow I didn't think I would feel very comfortable at that one. I read on. "Pedagogy and Pederasty: Rend(er)ing the Body in the Multi-gendered Classroom." With a panel of experts, I wondered? Then "Windows on the Womb: Voyeurism and Paranoia in Postsociety." Postsociety? I didn't know what that was. Next: "Hot Bodies in a Cool World: Masturbatory Fantasies and Sexual Murder in the Novels of Judith Delauney Platt." Possible, if only I knew who Judith Delauney Platt was, which I didn't. Finally: "Organizational Meeting of the Committee to Erect a Tomb of the Unknown Victim." No real interest there.

I nursed my drink as long as I could, and then, after the session started, I wandered aimlessly from one room to another looking in on the various meetings. The speakers were all perky, bright, fully convinced. No doubt? I wondered. No uncertainty? Evidently not. I didn't think I could stand to listen to any of them.

I took the stairway to the second floor, where there were some faculty offices and a small lounge. I sat by a window for a few minutes and listened to the rain fall outside. I was about to rise and drift about some more when I was startled by a loud crash, followed by the sound of someone moaning. It was coming from the office of a professor I knew. "Professor Reich," I called, "are you all right?" I listened. I could hear someone moving inside. "Professor Reich! Can you hear me? Are you hurt?" I didn't know what to do. I tried the door but it was locked. "Professor Reich," I said, "wait right there. I'll get someone to help."

I had taken only a few steps towards the stairs when I heard Professor Reich's voice call out, "Wait!"

"What?"

"Just wait."

About a minute later Professor Reich opened his door a few inches and peeked out. "Oh, Jones," he said. He was a tall burly man and I could see that his face was flushed and his scraggly hair was more than usually disheveled. The office was dark, and when I tried to look behind him he shifted about as if he were trying to hide something from view. "I've been meaning to talk to you, Jones," he said. "I'm having Professor Kerne and Professor Lathrop and some other friends of mine over for a party tonight, and I'd be very pleased if you could come. It would be an opportunity for you to make some very important contacts. Do say you'll make it."

"Well, yes," I said, "sure."

"Good. You know the address?"

"No."

"Here, I'll write it down for you," he said, and he reached out and took the program from my hand. As he did so, I caught a glimpse of what he had been trying so diligently to hide. A young man was sitting demurely on the couch with his hands folded in his lap and his eyes on the floor.

"There," the professor said. Then I thought of something.

"Ah..."

"Yes?"

"I just remembered that I'm meeting a friend of mine tonight."

"Well, are you doing anything in particular?"

"No."

"Then bring him along," he said and smiled and closed the door.

~

MY friend Alex had called that morning and said he needed to see me. Now we were walking uptown to Professor Reich's apartment. "You should have told me you were going to a conference," he said. "I would have gone with you."

"Well, you wouldn't have enjoyed it much."

"Oh, no. I guess you've got to be specialist or something."

"It's not that."

"Hey, I read books. *Moby-Dick* and all that. Don't think just because..."

"It's not that," I said. "It's just that there wasn't much to enjoy."

Alex looked at me for a moment. "Well that's a hell of a resounding endorsement. You mean you're finally getting tired of that graduate school bullshit? I knew you would."

"It's all right, I guess."

"Oh, bullshit! You think it's bullshit. I know you. I've known you all your life."

"All *your* life."

"Right. So give it up. Why waste your time?"

"Can't."

"Why not?"

"No money. You know. All I've got is that fellowship."

"Oh, hell, you can always find something. Look at me."

"That's different," I said.

We found Professor Reich's building and walked into the foyer. "Your professor's doing all right," Alex said.

We took the elevator up to a private entranceway. I pressed the buzzer and the door was opened by a startlingly handsome young man in black tie. Damn, I thought, I didn't know it was black tie. I stuck out my hand to say hello but the young man kept his hand on the door and shook his head minutely from side to side.

"I... ah..." I started again. The young man motioned for us to come inside. Damn, again, I thought. He's from the catering service.

It was a huge apartment, and we wandered through several rooms filled with people until we reached the library. Here we found Professor Reich, and he introduced us to a number of his friends, including Professor Kerne.

"I'm sure you remember his paper," Professor Reich said, "'The Anus as Signifier'?"

"Oh, yes," I lied. "I enjoyed it very much."

Professor Kerne waved his hands as if to show that it was nothing. "It was a simple idea, really," he said. "Most of the important research had been done for us already by our colleagues in feminist studies. If, as they had shown, the phallus, being essentially singular, was therefore divisive and exclusionary, and if, by contrast, the vagina was inclusive and therefore unifying, well, then, you've got two erotic centers accounted for, but where does that leave the anus?" He paused significantly.

"Out in the cold?" Alex said.

"Precisely!"

"Sort of swingin' in the breeze," Alex went on.

"Swinging in the breeze, indeed!" Professor Kerne laughed out loud. "Swinging in the breeze. That's *very* good!"

Alex asked me in a whisper, "Did he say the anus was a sphincter?"

"Signifier, you idiot."

"Oh," Alex said.

"What's that?" Professor Kerne asked.

"We were just saying," Alex replied, "that the anus is a signifier."

"Do you really think so?" Professor Kerne said.

"Oh yes," Alex said, "I've always thought that."

Professor Kerne became terribly interested in Alex's views on the subject and drew him some distance away so that they could continue their discussion alone.

"Your friend's made a good start," one of the other professors said to me.

"Kerne is an important man to know," said another.

"Where does your friend study?" asked the first.

"He doesn't," I said. "He's training to be a stockbroker."

The professors burst out laughing. They thought I was making a joke.

~

THE waiters never stopped bringing around trays loaded with food and drink, and in a short time everyone seemed pretty well drunk. It was raining hard outside. Professor Reich sat down next to me. "Where do you live, Jones?"

I told him.

"Oh, it will be terrible getting out there tonight. Why don't you stay here? We've got plenty of room."

"That's very kind," I said, "but I wouldn't want to trouble you."

"No trouble at all," he said, and he grabbed me by the thigh, on the inside, rather high up.

"It's all right," I said, "I can manage."

"Don't be ridiculous. I wouldn't think of it," he said, moving his hand up my crotch and squeezing me tight.

"No, really," I said, starting from my chair. "It's quite all right."

~

I DIDN'T see Alex for about another hour and when at last we met we slipped out of the party and hailed a taxi on the street. Once under way Alex said, "You get raped?"

"No."

"Christ, I almost did. That butt-man, or whatever his name was."

"Kerne."

"Yeah. Sphincter-man. That's a hell of a crowd you run around with."

"Sorry."

"Don't mention it. Hey, I got something for you." Alex shifted in his seat and reached into his pocket. It was a book. "Like it?"

I took a look at it. Virginia Woolf. First edition. Signed. "Where'd you get this?"

"What's it worth?"

"I don't know. About a thousand dollars."

Alex frowned in disappointment. "That all?" he said. "I thought it would be worth more than that. How about this?"

He handed me another. Thomas Wolfe. First edition. Signed. "What's that worth?"

"About the same."

"Christ," Alex said. "No wonder you're broke."

~

ALEX called me the next morning and asked me to meet him for breakfast. We were settled into our table and had started our coffee when Alex suddenly said, "Listen, why don't you take a vacation with me?"

"Can't."

"Why not?"

"No money. Besides, I'm in the middle of a term."

"Oh, it's almost over. It can't matter much if you miss a week or two."

"Well, it does."

"But you hate the stuff."

"Doesn't matter. It's what I do."

"Personally, I think it's all a fraud anyway."

"What?"

"All that crap about understanding poetry. I don't think you can do it. I don't think your professors can either. Come on. What do you say? Take a vacation with me."

"Why are you so hot on getting away?"

"I need a break. I've had enough of stockbrokering. I've got some vacation coming to me and I thought, you know, it would be fun. The two of us, we'll drive around, pick up babes, you know, do whatever we want."

"Sounds wonderful."

"Oh, don't get that way. Jesus Christ. Don't get that way. What? Are you saving yourself for marriage?"

"Perhaps."

"Let's change the subject," Alex said. But he didn't change the subject. He took a sip of his coffee and said, "Oh, by the way, I saw Sophia the other day."

"No."

"I did."

"Why would you be seeing Sophia?"

"I've always seen Sophia. Sophia's great. She's a great kid. I've always kept up with Sophia. She's working with a firm down on the Street and we have lunch about once a month."

"You never told me that."

"Well what's to tell ya, kid? I never see you, anyway."

"So how is she?"

"Sophia? She's great. Work's great. Her family's great. But as a matter of fact she spent most of the time talking about you."

"I almost believe that."

"She did. And you know what she said? She said, 'You know, I think I really missed something there with Jones.'"

"All right. Enough already."

"I mean it. She thinks she made a big mistake. She was really interested to hear what you were doing."

Sophia and I had dated for one month. Twenty-seven days, to be precise. That was the culmination of over two years in which I had abjectly adored her. Then she simply broke it off. I never understood what had happened, or if I had done anything wrong. She never gave me a reason. She simply said things weren't working out the way she thought they would. I had always worshipped her far too much to push her in any way, and there at the end of our relationship I didn't have the courage to press her for an explanation, either. I just kept hoping that she would change her mind, somehow, but she never did. For my part, I never could get over her. I always felt that she was my one true love and that I had missed my greatest chance at happiness. I knew Alex well enough to know he might be joking, but it was something I didn't feel like being joked about.

"So here's what I'm thinking," Alex went on. "Sophia's going to her parents' place to open it for the summer. Let's drive down, pay her a visit, and take things from there."

"I don't suppose the little matter of an invitation would hold you back."

"Oh, you know Sophia."

"And money?"

"We'll sell those books you've got."

"They're not ours."

"Sure they are."

"They're not."

"Whose are they then?"

"Professor Reich's, I suspect."

"Really? Call him up and find out."

"Anyway, we're not selling them."

"Well then let me have the goddamned things. You don't want to get your hands dirty? I'll sell them."

"No."

Alex sat back and shot his hands in the air. "You're not going to sell them and you're not going to give them back, so what the hell are you going to do with them?"

"I don't know." I thought for a minute. All I could say was, "I don't know how I'm going to face him."

"Then leave."

"I'm in the middle of a term."

"*And you fucking hate it!* Come on, wake up! What, are you going to spend the rest of your life doing stuff you don't want to do? Come on. For once in your life have some fun!"

~

I LED Alex down Madison Avenue to one of the oldest and most respected book dealers in the city. Alex sniffed around the polished mahogany shelves, looked the aged proprietor up and down, and then said in a voice loud enough for everyone to hear, "Won't take you long to get this place on its feet."

"I beg your pardon, sir."

Alex ignored him.

"Is there something I can do for you, sir?" the man persisted.

"Not now, thank you," Alex said. "We'll have a look 'round first."

Alex stopped before a photograph on the wall of the much younger owner standing in his shop surrounded by half a dozen famous writers. "Who are these people?" Alex asked me.

"W.H. Auden, Tennessee Williams…"

"Oh bullshit. You don't know."

"They're just writers."

"I've met just one writer in my life," Alex said. "Judy Wheaton, at a dinner. She puked."

The old man gave us a cold look.

"It was the salmon mousse. Made me sick too."

I leaned close to Alex's ear. "Aren't you going to show him the books?"

"Shush," he said. He looked up at the shelves and pulled down a volume. "*The Sexual Life of Savages*," he read out loud, "by B. Malinowski." He opened the book in the middle and read silently for a few moments. "*Really Very Disgusting!*" he exclaimed at last, slapping the book shut, and then, "Malinowski. That's a Jewish name, isn't it?"

The owner was glaring down at us pretty hard now, so I said, "Come on, let's go," and Alex followed me out of the shop.

"Well, that was a good bit of selling you did in there," I said when we were safely on the street.

"Your fault," Alex said.

"How so?"

"Too established. Incorruptible. Did it never occur to you that that old man might have known where these books came from? Might have sold them to your professor himself? No. We need something smaller. More hole-in-corner. Somewhere where they won't ask questions."

"All right," I said. I knew what he wanted.

I took Alex to a bookshop downtown with rather a different reputation. The owner, a bizarre looking woman in her mid-forties, was infamous for buying valuable old books and then tearing them page from page so that she could sell the individual sheets framed. She was able to make twenty times her money that way, but it was severely frowned upon. I had also heard from other book dealers that she was considered the worst person in the business to work for. I could have guessed that myself. I was once in her shop listening to her bossing around her young employees, as usual. Then she stepped outside for a moment, came back in, and shouted for everyone to hear, "Matthew! (or whatever his name was) There's *DOG SHIT* on the sidewalk. *CLEAN IT UP!*"

We reached the place and went inside. Alex looked 'round at the dusty piles of books and then at the owner behind the counter. Her hair was teased out in all directions and she was eating an egg salad sandwich and making a messy job of it.

"This looks like the place," Alex said. He walked up to the counter and said, "I'd like you to look at some books I have for sale."

"Put 'em down," she said, indicating the counter. She kept eating her sandwich with one greasy hand and with the other she pawed through the pages.

"They're inscribed, as you can see," Alex said.

"I can see it."

"I'm thinking about a thousand dollars each."

She slid them away from her and with a mouth full of sandwich said, "Keep 'em."

Alex slid them forward again. "The price can be negotiated. They have a lot of potential. The signatures can be taken out. The dust covers could be transferred to other copies. There are other possibilities…"

She pawed them around again. "Woolf's still in demand, but Thomas Wolfe's out of the picture."

"He's out of the pig shit?"

"He's out of the… I could give you one thousand for the both."

"I couldn't take less than one-five."

"Look, bud, I'm a dealer, not a collector. I only want 'em for what I can sell 'em for."

"Shall we say one-two-five? You'll make much more than that."

She ruminated for a moment. "Yeah. Okay. One-two-five." Alex smiled. She pushed aside some debris and started to write out a check. It seemed like a good price, but who knows?

As soon as we were back on the street Alex said, "You didn't tell me she was a lesbian."

"Is she?"

"Oh God! Worst I've ever seen."

"Does it make a difference?"

"Didn't this time. But it could have. It's better to know these things in advance."

We agreed to split up and meet the next day to drive down to the shore. Alex took the check to cash and said he'd pick up his car. I didn't have too clear of an idea of how all this would work out. By selling the books I'd pretty much sealed my fate with the graduate school. There was no going back now. That meant no fellowship, which meant no money. And I didn't believe Sophia wanted to see me. Or rather, I didn't want to believe it. I'd spent too many sleepless nights already. I couldn't afford any more. Nevertheless, at bottom, I knew Alex was right. I was stuck in a rut, and it was killing me. I needed to reach out and get a grip on life. This, at least, was a start.

~ *Chapter Two*

WITH ALEX DRIVING, we sped across the vast wasteland that separates the city from the ocean. It was a route we knew well, since our families, and most of the families we had grown up with, spent at least a part of every summer at the shore.

Our plan, as Alex had outlined it, was to arrive at Sophia's door and simply tell her we would like to spend a few days. It was true, as he said, that she would hardly send us packing; nonetheless, it struck me as odd. "Why don't we call her?" I asked. But Alex insisted that this was the way to do it.

We finally reached the long causeway that connects the mainland to the island. As we passed the top of the bridge and started down on the far side, I found myself becoming increasingly apprehensive at the prospect of meeting Sophia. Of course I would like to see her, but I didn't believe she wanted to see me. And it was obvious that she still had such command over my feelings that I would be mortified if she showed any sign of displeasure at our showing up unannounced. I felt that we were making a mistake.

Alex turned north onto the main road. The shore places were on our right and the bayside houses on the left. Sophia's house was a mile or so up on the right, so I expected Alex to speed along as usual until we were there, but he didn't. Rather, he slowed down and craned his neck forward and looked in both directions through the windshield as though he were searching for something.

"It's up ahead," I said.

He continued to drive slowly, and when at last the house came in view he followed it carefully with his eyes but drove past.

"That's it," I said.

"Oh," Alex said. He pulled over to the curb about two houses down the street, put the car into park and shut it off.

"Aren't you going to turn around?" I asked.

"No. This car steers like a pig," he said, rather inconsequentially. "We'll park here. This is fine."

We got out and started to walk back to the house, but here also Alex's mode of approach was unusual. He cut away from the road one driveway too soon and so we came upon Sophia's house through the back yard. When we were about fifty feet away, he stopped and surveyed the house carefully. "Damn," he said, "it doesn't look like anybody's here." My immediate feeling was one of relief. "Let's check it out and see if she's coming back," Alex said.

He crept forward and carefully opened the back screen and tried the door. Locked. He then walked around the house and looked in at each window. I followed him. "It doesn't look like she's been here at all," he said.

"No, it doesn't."

"Let's see if we can get inside."

"What do you mean?"

"You know. Climb in."

"You can't just break into someone's house," I said. "It's not right. In fact, it's against the law."

"Come on, it's only Sophia's house."

"No."

"What's the big deal? Either she hasn't been here and we'll know for sure, or she has and we'll stay and wait."

"Inside?"

"What?"

"Wait inside?"

"Inside, outside. It doesn't matter. Maybe outside." He made this last remark, I'm sure, to placate me. Meanwhile, he started on a second circuit of the house, trying each window as he went along. None were unlocked, but something about one of them attracted his interest. He started to bang and push on it.

"What are you doing?"

"Just shut up," he said.

After a minute or two of exertion something in the frame snapped and the window slid open. Alex climbed through. "Come on," he said. Reluctantly, I followed.

Once inside, Alex walked off down the hall, but I stood motionless and took a deep breath. I felt as though I had stepped back in time into a distant, long lost world. Memories that I had tried so hard to push out of my mind now came flooding over me. I glided over to the large, airy living room, the room in which I had spent the most exquisite, most anguished, and most horrible days of my life. Sophia's picture stood on the mantle. I went over and picked it up and looked once more into her face and was struck anew by its utter, almost unbearable beauty. I had once held that face, I thought to myself, even kissed it. I knew this to be a fact, but I now found it hard to believe. I picked up another picture: Sophia standing on the porch in a light summer dress. She had a perfect figure, one could see that, and yet I had hardly dared to touch her.

I sat down on the sofa. Here Sophia and I once sat talking and laughing, and here a few weeks after that Sophia had turned her face away and said she didn't want to be with me anymore.

I took another deep breath. For some reason sitting there like a thief in that silent, empty room I began to feel strangely at peace. All will be well, I said to myself. Everything is just as it had been. Our past was held by this room, and I knew then that I would always have had some part in Sophia's life, however small, and that nothing whatever could eclipse that.

I was interrupted in these pointless musings by a loud crash from one of the farther rooms, and by the voice of Alex, who said, "Shit!" I followed the commotion into Sophia's bedroom. Alex was in her closet, bent over and elbow-deep in a pile of boxes

"What are you doing?"

"Looking around."

"What for?"

"Just looking around. Sit down and relax."

I sat down on the bed. "Why can't you leave things alone?" I said.

"Why can't you shut up?"

"You know you came here as though you meant to break in," I said. "For all we know, Sophia might not be coming down here at all."

Alex didn't respond to this. He was rifling through a small accordion file on the floor of the closet. "Those look like personal papers," I said.

"It's just ordinary stuff."

I walked out of the bedroom and went to the kitchen to get a glass of water. I stood drinking by the window for several seconds or so before I realized with a shock that I was looking straight into the face of another man. "Mr. Zukofsky!" I said. It was the neighbor. We'd known him since we were children.

"Jones, is that you?"

"Yes!"

"What a relief, I—"

"Wait a minute," I said. I couldn't hear him too well. I went to the back door and let him in.

"What are you doing?" he asked.

I told him we were expecting to meet Sophia, but that we must have gotten the dates wrong.

"Sophia? Oh, no, the Westons aren't coming down for a couple of weeks yet. Nobody's here but us."

Alex came into the kitchen and said hello to Mr. Zukofsky.

"Well, you know I saw you two climbing into a window and I didn't know what to think."

"Yes, I don't know what went wrong," Alex said. "I was told Sophia would be here. Obviously she's not. It looks like we made the whole trip for nothing."

"Oh well, that happens. You boys have dinner yet? Why don't you come over and have dinner with us? Heck, well, you know, why don't you stay with us for a few days? You might as well. Lisa's coming in tonight. She's at Smith, you know." Lisa was his only daughter.

The Zukofsky's house was of a modern design, with vast plain white walls and thin lancet windows that reached from the ground to the roof, cutting through all three floors. The interior walls were also white and completely unadorned. There were no lamps that one could see, their function taken over by recessed spotlights set at curious angles in the ceiling and walls. At the far end of the entrance hall there was a large semi-circular staircase that connected the first and second floors. In the open area at the base rested a life-size bronze sculpture of what appeared to be a fat, naked woman squatting to relieve herself.

Mrs. Zukofsky was in the kitchen preparing a meal. "Well, hello," she called out. "How are you boys? It's so good to see you. How are your parents? When are they coming down? Have you seen Lisa, our big college girl? She's finishing her first year at Smith. Can you believe it? She's at Smith. Did you know that? She loves it. She's coming down for the weekend. Isn't that nice? You'll be able to see her. You won't recognize her, she's so grown up."

Mrs. Zukofsky was a rather heavy-set woman, and she was wearing a colorful, flowing robe as if she were the priestess of some exotic cult. On a heavy marble table she set out grass mats, four broad, flat, stoneware bowls, cups, a pitcher of water, and black lacquered chopsticks. Then, on a large serving platter, she brought us what appeared to be raw fish wrapped in seaweed, small bunches of bean sprouts tied with strips of bamboo, and small dumplings filled with rice and some type of edible flower. These were served cold, as I imagine they were meant to be, and Mrs. Zukofsky instructed us to dip them into a brown sauce that she set out in another bowl.

Mrs. Zukofsky was very interested to learn that I was at the university. "I just took a course there," she said. "Deconstruction and Architecture. Gafflin. Professor Gafflin. Do you know him?"

"No."

"It was such a great course. We studied everything. But, oh, it was so expensive."

"I didn't know."

"Over fourteen thousand dollars!"

"Fourteen...for...what? A year?"

"No, a course. Fourteen thousand dollars for a course. It's—what do you call it?—it's on-site learning. It's on-site. You can't learn anything in a classroom. You have to go there. Paris, Rome, we went everywhere. Have you been to Rome?"

"No," I said, "but I've been to Paris."

"Paris," she said disdainfully, "has got *nothing*. I wouldn't even waste my time in Paris. Rome! Rome is the place you have to go for architecture."

"It sounds like a great course," I said.

"Our professor introduced us to all the latest theories—you know, Derint and Lintzer?"

I hadn't heard of them, but I played along.

"Well, do you know what they proved? It's all castration anxiety! Did you know that? It's all castration anxiety! It's all a what do you call it?" She strained for the words. "It's a compensation for male insecurities. That's why men build these big tall buildings—to compensate for their castration anxiety. I mean you're looking at this building, and all of sudden it hits you that it's just a big penis! It's really just a great big penis! Isn't that fascinating?"

"What did your classmates think?"

"Well, you know there was this one lady in our group from Chicago and she said she didn't think that could explain everything. And you know, something in the way she said it made me think. And then it hit me, like a big, I don't know what, like a big flash, and I realized what it was. They're not as sophisticated! From Chicago. They're not as sophisticated as we are, because we're from the east, and that makes us more sophisticated, you know, like with abortion and divorce and capital punishment and everything. But in Chicago, they're not as sophisticated."

Mr. Zukofsky and I caught each other's eye, exchanged meaningless glances and kept eating, but Alex picked up the ball. "I see exactly what you mean," he said. "We're definitely more sophisticated. I've been to Chicago and I know exactly what you mean."

We finished our meal and Mrs. Zukofsky cleared our places. She told us that the next course she was taking was on Virginia Woolf. "You know everything comes from Virginia Woolf. Everything. Modernism and, you know, the whole modern way of doing things. She started all that."

"Is it on-site?" I asked.

"No," she said, as though she couldn't quite see the point in the question. Then she looked at the clock and said that we'd have to excuse her because her favorite television show, "Culture Vultures," was about to begin.

Mr. Zukofsky made us each a drink, and we took these and moved into the living room. The furniture was all rather low, wide, and shapeless and it was hard to make oneself comfortable trying to sit. Once you got the idea, however, that you were only supposed to slump, then it was all right. We all slumped back in our chairs. Unfortunately, this meant that we couldn't really look at each other as we talked, because all of our faces were aimed at the ceiling. This did bring into prominence, however, the only bit of ornament in the room. Above the fireplace, which was itself no more than a rectangle cut into the wall, there hung a large abstract painting of wild, angry, and conflicting colors.

"Oh, what a great picture!" Alex said.

"You like it?" Mr. Zukofsky asked.

"Oh, yeah, definitely. Where'd you get it?"

"The Sutherland Gallery. In the city."

"How much?"

Mr. Zukofsky balked at this for a moment, and then said, "Fifteen thousand."

"You stole it."

"You think so?"

"Definitely."

Mr. Zukofsky had always been a gentle, quiet, long-suffering man, and he clearly appreciated this comment. He settled deeper in his chair and said, "It's funny how we got it. A guy in the firm had invitations to an opening because his daughter was a friend of the artist. Well, we didn't have anything to do so we thought it would be fun. We got to meet the artist, and Sally [that was Mrs. Zukofsky] really took a liking to her. She and her husband were there and they'd just had this little baby, you know, and you could tell they didn't have much money. So I saw this one and I said Sally let's buy it, and, would you believe it, this was the one she wanted, too."

"It's a great picture," Alex said.

"It's funny, though. After we bought it I kind of thought we ought to have another one to go on the other side of the room. So we called her up and she asked us to come to her studio. Well, she called it her studio, but really all three of them lived in this one room on the lower east side. Most of the room they gave to the baby. I think they slept on the couch. Well, anyway, she pulled out some pictures but there was nothing like this. She said with the baby it was hard to work and even this one here she painted before the baby was born. But then I saw these three small paintings hanging over the baby's crib. All the same: sort of fuzzy lines of white and blue and gold. They were very peaceful, very pretty, you know. They looked like the beach, like here. So I asked her what about those? But she said, oh no, they're not for sale, she only made those so the baby would have something pretty to look at. So I asked her if she could make me some just like them. And you know what she said? She said she couldn't do it. The pictures weren't serious enough. Well, I really wanted them now, so I told her I'd pay her twenty thousand dollars for the set but she said no. So then I said I'd pay her twenty thousand dollars just to do one, and she said no, her conscience wouldn't allow it. I was really floored. I mean they were practically starving. It wouldn't have taken her more than a day or two at the most. I mean, heck, I'd like to make that kind of money. But she wouldn't do it. She absolutely refused. I'll never forget it." He took a sip of his drink, looked up at the painting and then back at each of us. He shrugged his shoulders and smiled. "I guess that's the way they are, artists," he said. "Free spirits."

"Well, I think you got the best one of the bunch," Alex said. Mr. Zukofsky got up to refill our glasses. When he returned, Alex said, "Now about this sculpture under the stairs…" but he was interrupted by the sound of a car coming up the drive. It was Lisa.

Mrs. Zukofsky was quite right: Lisa was all grown up and was really quite attractive. She was smartly dressed, had long straight dark hair, and moved in a lithe, confident manner. She gave her father a big hug and kiss and made a big fuss over him. Her mother yelled a hello from the bedroom and Lisa raised her eyebrows the slightest fraction of an inch and then went in to say hello to her mother. We sat down again and in a short while Lisa came back to join us. She sat next to her father and took his arm. Everything in her manner suggested that she was more comfortable around men.

We talked about school, and Lisa was interested to learn that I was studying literature. Literature, she said, was her favorite subject. "Do you use beach balls?" she asked.

"No, I don't think so."

"We do. Our professor has us sit around a big round table and if anyone wants to talk you have to throw them the beach ball. You can't talk unless you have the beach ball."

"That's an interesting system."

She told us a lot of other things, too, about what books she had read and what concerts and lectures she had gone to. "Which Balinese poets do you like the most?" she asked. I had to admit I didn't know any. Then suddenly she stood up, stretched herself, and began to wander around the room as if to reacquaint herself with her surroundings. She drifted off to the kitchen, opened the refrigerator, took out a beer, called in to see if we needed anything, and then came back and sat down again, this time next to Alex.

She asked what was on television but no one knew so she picked up the remote control and turned on the set. First there was a news program about a man who weighed one thousand three hundred pounds then lost seven hundred and then gained back four hundred. They took him to the hospital using a forklift. His wife fed him twenty-four deep-fried breaded pork chops and three pounds of mashed potatoes every night. When the commercials came on, Mr. Zukofsky made his excuses and got up to go to bed.

Next there was a segment about a firehouse dog who during his long career had saved the lives of many people but who recently had been struck by a car and killed. A memorial service was held in his honor attended by the mayor, who spoke of the dog's courage and loving, caring nature. The dog's bereaved owner, a burly fireman, wept openly. A microphone was thrust in the man's face. "He shall be missed!" was all the poor man could manage to sputter through his tears.

"God, you hate to see that," Lisa said.

"I know," said Alex. "It's so sad."

They seemed prepared to expand on the subject, so I excused myself and asked where we would be staying. Lisa pointed to a door just off the living room.

I undressed and looked for something to read, but there was nothing. I got under the covers, turned off the light and lay on my back and tried to think. Something was not right. Alex had been acting quite strangely, but really no more than on many other occasions. Nobody ever really understood him. He always kept his friends and family in the dark about most things, and he had certainly made his share of mistakes in life. Nonetheless, as he never tired of telling me, he was my oldest friend, and, for better or worse, I imagined he always would be.

Somewhere in the midst of these reflections I suppose I fell asleep, for in what seemed a short time after someone was shaking me awake. It was Alex.

"You have to get up."

"What? Why?"

"Go over to Lisa's room. It's next door to her parents'."

I looked around. Lisa was standing at the door in her panties holding her shirt in front of her.

"We need to use this room," Alex explained.

I was totally at a loss. Lisa made an impatient gesture with her hand. There wasn't much I could say. I got up, put on my trousers, and started across the living room to the bedrooms on the other side. "It's the one on the left," Lisa said. I found it, climbed into bed, and fell asleep.

A moment later, I was being shaken awake again.

"Get up. Your turn."

"What?" It was Alex.

"She's waiting."

He was completely naked. He bent over me and breathed in my ear, "C'mon. I talked her into it."

"Into what?"

"She wants it. C'mon. She's waiting for you." He nodded towards the door.

I was wide awake now. "Are you insane?"

"No, I'm serious. She wants it. She's into it."

I sat up straight and pushed Alex away from me. "You're sick, Alex."

"Oh, come on."

"The answer is no. I can't believe you. We're guests here."

This last remark failed to register. "You don't want her?"

"No."

"You sure?"

"Yes."

"Okay. Sorry. Go back to sleep."

I was woken again, but it was morning. A dim light filled the room, and I could hear birds outside. Lisa was standing by the bed in her underwear. "You can go back now," she said. I got up, gathered my things, and walked back to the other end of the house.

~

THE Zukofsky's gave us breakfast in the morning along with advice on how to contact the Westons and find Sophia. Alex seemed a good deal tired and out of sorts. It was obvious he wasn't paying a bit of attention. We thanked everyone and said goodbye and started towards the car. Just as we were getting in Alex turned back and exchanged a quick word with Lisa. Then he climbed in, started the engine, and headed down the main road.

"Well, you really missed something," Alex said.

"I don't want to hear about it."

"She's absolutely a wild woman."

"I don't want to hear about it."

"You can't believe what she—"

"Shut up," I said. "I've told you I don't want to hear about. If you want to act like an animal, that's your business. I don't have to hear about it. All I can say is that it was very, very wrong."

"But she wanted it."

"It was wrong to her parents."

"How so?"

"We were guests there."

"I don't see how that makes any difference."

"Well, if you can't see it, you can't."

He let the matter drop and drove on in silence. Then, after several minutes, he said, "I don't care what Mr. Zukofsky said, Sophia is down here."

"How do you know?"

"I just know."

"So what do you suggest?"

"Just keep looking 'til we find her. She's here somewhere."

The morning air was cool and I was still somewhat sleepy. I wrapped my arms around myself, snuggled back in my seat, and closed my eyes. "Whatever you think best," I said.

~ *Chapter Three*

WE DROVE ALONG the shore to where Sophia's cousins had a house, but it was all shut up. Then we remembered a clothing store where an old friend of Sophia's had once worked. The store was open, but the people there didn't remember either Sophia or her friend. Then, for a change of pace, we drove farther south to a town with a boardwalk and a penny arcade. We played skeeball and shot pellet rifles at paper targets. We ate lunch at a sausage shop on the boardwalk, and then by late afternoon decided to look for a bar.

On a side street we found a dark, tumbled-down place with a long row of motorcycles outside. "This looks interesting," Alex said. Inside, there were a dozen or so bikers, some at the bar and others scattered about at different tables. They were rough-looking types, with long hair and leather jackets and long scraggly beards. Loud music blared from a jukebox in the corner, and the atmosphere was rich with the stench of urine and rancid beer.

"You're kidding," I whispered to Alex.

"No. Come on. This place is great."

We found space at the bar and Alex ordered two Blue Maxes.

"What's that?" the bartender asked.

"Rum, 151, lighted with a match."

"Lighted with a match?"

"That's right."

"I got to charge you extra to light it," the bartender said, which I took to be his way of telling us to get lost.

"Well, you got to do what you got to do," Alex said.

The bartender went away to get our drinks and I whispered to Alex, "He's going to light our drinks on fire?"

"Yeah."

"I'll take mine without, if you don't mind."

"Oh, come on, you've got to. You got to show these guys you're as tough as they are. You don't want them to think we're pussies, do you?"

"I don't care what they think."

The bartender returned with our drinks and lit them. The bikers stopped what they were doing and watched as Alex lifted the shot-glass with its ghostly blue flame, put it to his lips, and drank. Then he looked at me. This was so stupid, I thought. "Come on," Alex urged in a whisper. "You don't want them to think you're a wuss. Come on."

I put my fingers around the glass. It was warm at the top. I accidently jiggled it a bit and some of the rum spilled out and splashed in a blue flame over the bar. Well, we really had their attention now. I put the burning liquid to my mouth, thought discordantly of the ancient Romans, and in one rapid gulp swallowed it down.

"Very good," Alex said, with a proud, approving smile.

As it turned out, no one was really very impressed. After only a moment they all turned back to their own business. The front door swung open and two slutty-looking girls came in off the street and sat down at a table.

I suppose we had earned our place at the bar, but for some reason this was not enough for Alex. He ordered two more drinks and set himself to listening to the conversation of the group of bikers nearest to us.

"Here's to the Skinner," one of them said.

"Here's to the Skinner," they all said, and raised their glasses and drank.

"Here's to the Skinner!" Alex said loudly, and did the same.

The bikers turned to look at us again, and the largest and filthiest of them said, "What the hell you think you're doing, boy?"

"I'm drinking to this gentleman the Skinner," Alex said.

"And what the hell do you know about *him?*"

"Nothing," Alex said, "but if you gentlemen are drinking to him, I guess he's all right."

"All right? All right? He was more'n goddam' all right," the biker said. "The Skinner was fightin' god-damn gooks when scummy little punks like you were still suckin' tit. The gov'ment say he's MIA, but he ain't no MIA, he's POW. Charlie's got him. Got him prisoner. And we drinkin' to him every god-damn night till we get 'im back. Here. Alive."

"Gee," Alex said, "how long has Charlie had him?" I didn't know what Alex was driving at. He knew as well as I did that the war had been over for twenty-five years. "I mean, how do you know Charlie's still got him?"

The biker looked at Alex hard and then stood square in front of him as if he were ready for a fight.

"You ever been in a combat zone, son? You ever done any fighting?"

"The only fighting I've ever done was getting to a bar at closing time," Alex said.

The biker laughed. "That's all right," he said. The others laughed. "You get in a war, boy, you get to know your enemy. You get to know the way he thinks." The biker pointed vaguely in the direction of his head as if to indicate where thinking might take place. "Charlie's got his ass. That's the way Charlie's mind works. He'll take a man and he'll torture a man for the rest of his god-damn life. Shit. People say we lost that war. We didn't lose that war. Hell of a lot a dead Charlies wisht we lost that war."

The other bikers said, "Ah-huh" and "Damn right."

"We kicked their butts good," the biker went on. "That's why Charlie'll keep the Skinner and a lotta other good Americans for the rest of their lives until we get 'em back."

"I agree with you one-hundred percent," Alex said.

The two sluts had been listening to this exchange. One was a buxom bleach-blonde wearing blue jeans and a t-shirt so tight it was ready to burst. The other was sunken-eyed and emaciated, with greasy brown hair that hung straight down and seemed to adhere to her face. All during the biker's story Alex had been sneaking glances at them. Now, while the bikers were having their drinks refilled, Alex tried to catch their eye. He wasn't too subtle about it, and he was found out.

"You're not trying to pick up on our women, are you boy?" the large biker said.

"No sir, I am not."

"Good. Don't touch a man's bike and don't touch a man's bitches and you might live long enough to grow hair on your balls."

"Thanks for the tip," Alex said. "Hey, I bet you had a lot of women in the war."

"Oh, man," the biker said, "there was whores everywhere! Company Sergeant 'ud say we had to stay away from 'em 'cause they were all Charlie spies, then he'd hide in the bush and bang two or three of 'em at once. Yeah, I remember one time I was on perimeter duty and this old whore comes up and asks me if I want some ass. So I say no 'cause I'm on duty, you know. So the whore starts walking away from me, she's 'bout as far as from here to that wall over there, and then she picks up her dress, picks it right up to here and squats down like this and takes a big ol' shit right in the middle of the road. Just like that, man. I couldn't believe it. And I thought, damn, man, I was almost in that! I was almost in that! I couldn't believe it." Alex and the other bikers laughed like crazy.

"That's a charming story," I whispered under my breath.

"What's that?" the biker said.

"Nothing," I said, and tried to smile. Alex bought them all a round of drinks and then said, "Boy, I've got to take a leak." He went down a dark passageway that led to the bathroom. A minute or two later the blonde followed him. Alex reappeared soon after, came back to the bar and whispered in my ear, "It's all set."

"What is?"

"The girls. They're gonna meet us."

"What for?"

Alex rolled his eyes and then concentrated on his drink. "Just relax and blend into the woodwork," he said. "We'll go in about a minute or two. They'll meet us in five minutes at the end of the street." Oh God, I thought, not again.

We left the bar and waited at the corner until the girls

showed up. Then the four of us scurried around to the next street to where we had parked our car. Alex unlocked the doors and introduced the two of us and asked them their names. The blonde was Dawn and the thin one was Tiffany. We got in and Alex started to drive. "What do you say?" he said, "Should we pick up something to drink?"

"Sure," Dawn said.

"You college guys?" Tiffany asked.

"Yeah," Alex said.

"Us too," Tiffany said.

"Oh."

"We're not like those guys at the bar," Dawn said. "We got ambitions."

"I could see that," Alex said.

"Those other guys, they don't want to do nothin' but drink all day," Dawn said.

"We're learnin' be witches," Tiffany said, in all seriousness.

"Really?"

"Yeah."

"Is that what you went to college for?" I asked.

"Yeah, what d'ya think?" Tiffany said, rather insulted.

"We only took one course," Dawn said. "We signed up for Bestiality but they told us we had to do all this reading so we didn't. One book was this fat." She held her thumb and forefinger three inches apart for me to see.

"It's not to everyone's taste," I said.

Alex was sensing trouble. He attempted to change the subject. "What are you doing next?"

"We're going to Africa," Dawn said. "We're gonna learn about the earth-mother. They have a whole school there."

"Africa," Alex said. "No kidding? My friend here has been to Africa. He speaks eleven African languages and he's eaten human flesh twice."

"Wow!" the girls said.

"Say something in African to them," Alex said.

Oh God! I thought, this is so stupid.

"Go on," Alex said.

"*O seclum insipiens et infacetum,*" I said.

"What's that mean?"

I thought for a moment. "It means I would like to pick up these shirts on Friday." Dawn was impressed, but Tiffany looked at me rather skeptically.

"What's Africa like?" she asked.

"Well, that depends where you go."

"We're going to Guyana."

"Guyana's in South America," I said.

"It's not in America!" she snapped indignantly. "We've seen it in the brochures." Once again she was insulted.

"My friend's just joking," Alex said. "He knows where Guyana is."

We stopped at a liquor store and asked the girls what they would like. They wanted beer. We chose a couple of six packs but the girls insisted on our buying quart bottles instead. It's easier that way, they said. That way everybody has their own. It's always impossible, they said, to divide a couple of six packs between four people. We didn't argue with them. We paid for eight quart bottles and each of us walked out of the store with the neck of a bottle in each fist.

"Shall we rent a room somewhere and have a party?" Alex asked. Oh, God, no, I thought. Thankfully, they said they'd rather party on the beach.

"Have you ever swam naked in the sea during a full moon?" Dawn asked.

"Yes!" Alex said. "I love that!"

I don't think he had, but he said it anyway. We parked the car and walked across the beach. We took off our shoes and got our feet wet. It was too cold to swim. I didn't bother to point out that it wasn't a full moon either. We sat on the sand and drank and smoked cigarettes and then before you know it Alex and Dawn were lying on the sand and making out. They started taking off each other's clothes.

"Dawn!" Tiffany cried, "do you know what you're doing?"

Dawn ignored her. I picked myself up and moved away from them down the beach. Tiffany stayed behind and circled around the couple and looked in here and there and said over and over, "Dawn, do you know what you're doing?" and "Dawn, do you know what he's doing to you?" I don't think Dawn was especially drunk or senseless; she simply chose not to respond. Tiffany walked back over the sand to where I was and plunked herself down in a huff. She shook her head. "I can't believe her," she said. She looked back several times and then got up to investigate some more, but she didn't come quite as close this time. All she could say over and over again was, "Dawn, do you know what you're doing?" It was incredibly boring. When she came back I tried to engage her in conversation but she seemed to think I was trying to seduce her and so she went off again in a huff. She wandered over to the couple on the sand, but this time she simply stood there and didn't say a thing. They were both completely naked now, and I couldn't help feeling that her interest was somewhat salacious.

I was getting tired and thought I might go back to the car to sleep, but then I remembered that the doors were locked and that Alex had the keys. Oh, well. I lay flat on my back and tried to get comfortable. Tiffany came over and sat down about ten feet away. "I can't believe her," she said for about the twentieth time. I looked up at the stars and tried not to think of anything at all. In a short while I was asleep.

I woke up and felt a hand going over my chest and a leg going over my thigh. I turned my head and saw that it was Tiffany. "I'm cold," she said, and I think she was. I let her snuggle against me and I went back to sleep.

I woke again and felt Tiffany's hand exploring my chest and stomach and then down over my pants. I looked at her. "You wanna fuck?" she said.

"No, thank you," I said, "I'm really very tired."

She didn't seem unnaturally offended by this. She stopped feeling me up, and in a short time I was asleep again. When I next awoke she was gone. The sun was coming up. I propped myself on my elbows and looked out over the ocean. Alex was bending over washing his hands and face in the sea. He turned and waved and walked up the beach. When he reached where I was he sat down and we both looked out over the water.

"You can't believe what happened."

"Don't tell me."

"You can't believe it—"

"Don't tell me!"

"No, it's not what you think."

"Then I'm sure I don't want to know."

"No, just listen to this. I was trying to undress her, you know? She had on one of those bras that clip in the front. So there I am reaching around trying to undo her bra when all of a sudden she sits straight up and gets all stiff. So I ask her what's wrong and she says 'I felt something.' What? 'I don't know.' Well, I didn't know what to make of that so I went back to work when all of a sudden she does it again. 'I feel something,' she says. What? 'I don't know.' It was weird. So finally I get her damned bra off, and then, when I lie back, I see that the cigarette I was holding in my teeth had burned a set of little black holes right in the middle of her back. And she didn't even feel it!"

"Yes," I said, "one could tell she was the sensitive type."
"Oh, she was a pig. Let me tell you—"
"Don't!"
"How'd you make out with yours?"
"Just fine."
"You nail her?"
"No, I did not 'nail her.' I slept."
"You didn't do anything?"
"No."
"You're kidding me."
"She asked me once if I wanted to have sex, but I said no."

Alex looked at me incredulously. Then he looked out over the ocean. "Whatever," was all he said.

We left the beach and found a diner and had breakfast and tried to make up our minds what to do next. We agreed that it was worthwhile to try to find Sophia, but I insisted once again that the most sensible thing would be simply to call her.

"Well, I have a confession to make," Alex said. "I have tried to call her, for several days, but I haven't been able to reach her."

"Have you tried her family?"

"No, but I don't want to try her family. I just don't feel like talking to them. Besides, she'd never be staying with her family. She has her own apartment."

"But you said she'd be staying with her family here."

"Well, that's what somebody told me."

"Who was that?"

"Someone—you don't know her—someone in the office who knows her. A friend of hers."

"And she said Sophia was going to her parents' house?"

"Yes."

I thought for a moment. "Is it possible," I said, "that when this friend of yours said that Sophia was going to her parents' house you thought she meant the beach house when really she meant the country house?"

This had clearly not occurred to him. He looked up at me, scrunched up his face, and then slowly drawled, "That could be."

"So the thing to do is try her at her country house."

"Yes. We could take a drive up there."

"I mean try her by calling her."

"Oh, we don't have to do that," Alex said. "Besides, even if we don't reach her on the phone, we'd still need to drive up to make sure."

"Do yourself a favor," I said. "Call."

Alex made a call from the phone booth but when he came back he told me there was no answer. We finished our breakfast, paid our bill, and left. It would be a good three hours' ride into the country. As before, Alex drove. I thought I should make some conversation.

"Did you ever hear of a book," I asked him, "called *The Slutting of Society?*"

"No."

"You should take a look at it. I think you'd find it interesting."

"What's it about?"

"It's about how social standards deteriorate. The idea is that when different levels of society come into contact, it is always the lower that drags down the higher, and not the reverse."

"Which would be the higher dragging down the lower."

"No, the higher elevating the lower."

"But surely—"

"You might well ask. Surely the higher society might already be falling on its own, but in the end the result is always the same: that the general level of civilization after the contact is always lower than it was before."

"That's if you believe there is a higher and a lower."

"Of course there is."

"Says who?"

"It's obvious. After all, intelligence is certainly quantifiable. Morality is too."

"Well, that's all very interesting," Alex said, "but you can't stop people from doing what they want."

"Oh, yes, you can," I said. "It's quite easy. You simply have to put your foot down."

"So you're telling me that people from different social levels shouldn't mix?"

"I'm telling you that people should maintain their standards. There's a difference."

We drove on for another half an hour and then Alex leaned forward and squinted ahead through the windshield. There were a couple of girls up the road hitch-hiking. "Babe alert!" he said, and started to slow down.

"Don't even think of it," I said. "Really, Alex. No."

Alex pulled alongside the girls, looked them up and down, seemed to reflect for a moment, then hit the accelerator and sped on. What a relief, I thought. And a vindication.

"There. You see," I said, "you can do it."

"What?"

"Maintain standards. You resisted doing what you thought you wanted to do."

Alex looked over at me. "No, I didn't. They were dogs so I figured let 'em walk."

"Oh, yes," I said. "Not quite up to your usual standards. Now that woman you were with last night, there was an enticing creature."

"That girl last night?"

"Dawn, I believe her name was."

"That woman was a pig. Let me tell you what she—"

"That's enough," I said. I held up my hand in a peremptory gesture.

"What? You don't like the way I go around with women?"

"Let's just say I don't think you should make it a settled principle."

"And what about you?"

"What about me?"

"You don't sleep with women?"

I paused for a second to reflect and then said, "I wouldn't mind sleeping with the woman I'm in love with. Unfortunately at the moment that woman does not love me."

"You never slept with Sophia?"

"That's none of your business."

"Don't tell me you don't sleep with anyone anymore."

"That is not a thing," I said, "that a gentleman will discuss."

"All right, all right, I got you," he said and laughed.

But something in our conversation did get him. He was silent for a long time, and rarely responded to my questions.

~ Chapter Four

WE REACHED SOPHIA'S house by lunchtime. No one was home. "I suppose now you'll want to break in," I said.

"Let's just have a look around."

"I'll wait in the car."

I didn't bother to watch. Alex returned in about twenty minutes. "She's not here," was all he said.

"Has she been here?"

"I don't think so."

Alex sat in the driver's seat and stared into the distance and tapped nervously with his fingertips on the steering wheel. He seemed to be thinking hard, but he didn't say anything. I started to wonder about things myself. Something was not right.

"Let's get something to eat," I said.

I knew the area better than Alex did, and I directed him to a diner in the next town. I waited until we had ordered our meal and then I excused myself to go wash up. The telephones were in an alcove hidden away from the tables. I dialed directory assistance and asked for the number of Sophia's parents in the city and then asked to be put through. Sophia's mother answered the phone.

"Hello, Mrs. Weston," I said, "this is Sophia's friend Jones. May I speak to Sophia?"

"Tom," she said, "is that you?"

"Yes."

"Have you seen Sophia?"

"No."

"Tom, we don't know where she is. We haven't heard from her in days. You haven't seen her?"

"No."

"Have you seen Alex?"

"No," I lied.

"Tom, I think they're in some kind of trouble. We called Alex's office and they say he's been fired, and Sophia hasn't been at work for over a week. They won't tell us anything more. We don't know what to do. You haven't seen her?"

"No," I said. "I was just calling to say hello. I tried her apartment, but there was no answer."

"Tom, if you see Alex would you ask him to call?"

"Yes, of course," I said.

"And you'll let us know if you hear anything?"

"Yes, of course."

"Please do, Tom. We're very worried."

We exchanged goodbyes and hung up.

I walked back to our table and sat down and looked at Alex. Our coffee had arrived and he was holding his cup in the air and staring out of the window. We sat there silently for a while.

"Well," I said, "as long as we're here, we might as well see what we can find out. Sophia has some friends in the area. They might know something."

"Who?" Alex asked, in an abstracted way.
"Sarah Dickson."
"She doesn't live here."
"She does now. She's moved in with Richard Atlee."
"She's going out with Richard Atlee?"
"She's living with him."

Alex groaned. "If I have to see that asshole just to talk to Sarah, then forget it."

"There's Charlie Morison," I said. "He used to date Sophia. He might know something."

Alex lit a cigarette. An old woman at the next table curled up her nose and waved her hand in front of her face and then leaned towards Alex and said, "Pardon me, young man, but I believe this is a nonsmoking area."

"Fuck you!" Alex said.

I paused to see what would happen, but she didn't say anything more.

"Fucking puritans," Alex said, "try to run your life."

"You really want to find Sophia?" I asked.

"Yeah. Sure. You want to see her, too, don't you?"

"Yes. So we'll check with Charlie Morison?"

"You think so?"

"Yes."

"Okay by me," Alex said.

The Morisons lived on a large estate called Wetherby. It had been in their family for centuries and had been declared a national historic site. Unfortunately, the family hadn't had the wherewithal to maintain the house for a very long time. Everyone who knew them urged them to sell it, either privately or to the state, before the building fell down completely, but they wouldn't hear of it.

We drove past the great stone gatehouse with its ornate ironwork and after another half a mile turned left onto a dirt road. This was the service entrance. The house was in such a condition of disrepair that the family had been forced to live in the servants' quarters for as long as anyone could remember. They opened the big house only on special occasions.

The drive was full of potholes and here and there a bush or a branch of a tree impeded our passage. The servants' quarters, when we reached them, resembled a series of chicken coops. There were three low, narrow structures on one side of the road, and two on the other. Alex brought the car to a halt and shut off the engine. It was deathly quiet. The sun was directly overhead, and the silence was made all the more profound by the constant droning of horseflies in the air. The atmosphere reminded me of nothing so much as some huts I had seen once in Jamaica. One expected to see the sullen gleam of eyeballs, perhaps human, perhaps animal, peering from out of the dark, blank, empty windows.

"What do we do?" Alex asked in a whisper.

"I don't know." The place seemed deserted, but all the same one had the sense that there were creatures everywhere hiding in the shadows.

"Hello!" I called out. "Is anybody there?"

There was no response but the droning of the horseflies.

I walked off towards the main house, one white corner of which I could just make out through the trees. I looked down several paths that led off from the main trail, but could see nothing. I walked back to the car and Alex and I exchanged helpless expressions. Then, quite unexpectedly, Alex turned and thrust his arm into the car and hit the horn and held it. The blaring of the horn and the heat from the sun overpowered my senses. I almost toppled off of my feet. Then it was over, and we got into the car and drove away without saying another word.

We cruised down the road and after a while the familiar scenery brought back memories and details I had forgotten. I suddenly realized why no one was home.

"They're probably at the stand," I said.

"What?"

"The Morisons. They keep a vegetable stand and sell produce from their farm."

"You're kidding?"

"No."

"The oldest family in the country, and they run a vegetable stand?"

"It's not their fault," I said.

Alex circled back to the highway, and soon at a widening of the road we saw a ramshackle wooden hut with a tiny gravel lot in front of it. Alex pulled in too quickly and had to brake hard, skidding on the stones and raising a cloud of dust.

The stand was open, and we could see Charlie's younger sister Pamela and another girl peering out. "Hello, Jones!" Pamela said when I got out of the car. "What are you doing here?" Pamela was a pretty blond girl of about fifteen. Her friend was dark-haired and quite attractive.

"We're just traveling," I said. "How have you been?

Pamela introduced her friend, whose name was Clarissa, and I introduced Alex. We chatted a bit before I noticed that they had their schoolbooks spread out on a table inside the hut. "Homework?" I asked.

"Yes."

"How's it going?"

"Oh, terrible," Pamela said. "We were doing history, but it was so stupid we had to stop. Our teacher used to be the driver's ed teacher but they put him in history because our last teacher quit."

"We drove her insane," Clarissa said.

"It's true," Pamela said. "We did. We went to visit her in the hospital last week and she screamed."

"It's a sad case," Clarissa added wistfully.

"Our new teacher told us he didn't know any history, but he Xeroxed all of his old notes and that's what he gives us to read."

"Not really?"

"Yes. His old high school notes."

"He makes a lot of spelling mistakes," Clarissa said.

"He asked us to stay after class today," Pamela said, "and told us that if we stopped correcting him so much in front of the rest of the class he'd give us both As. We've been sitting here trying to decide what 'too much' means. I think it means once a week. Clarissa thinks it means once every five minutes." She looked at me and raised her eyebrows and smiled. "So what do we do?"

"Well, that depends," I said.

"On what?"

"On whether you want to drive him insane or not."

Pamela pretended to think this over for a moment and said, "He's really rather a nice man," to which Clarissa replied, "He weighs three hundred pounds and smells like a hog."

"Then you'll have to compromise," I said. "And besides, you don't want to be cruel."

Pamela nodded in agreement while Clarissa turned up one corner of her mouth in a mischievous way and said, "Hmmm."

They were cute kids, and, I imagined, indeed more intelligent than their teacher. Then I asked Pamela if she knew where we could find Charlie.

"He's away," she said. "He's at some skateboarding race."

"A what?"

"A skateboarding race. He made some team and he's sort of semi-pro."

"Really?"

"Oh, it's horrible."

"They go seventy-five miles an hour," Clarissa said.

"On a skateboard?"

"Don't tell me!" Pamela said, putting her hands to her ears.

"On a skateboard," Clarissa repeated, and smiled.

All of this time Alex hadn't said anything, but when I looked at him I could tell that he was completely captivated by Clarissa. He smiled at her slightly and gazed at her face and laughed politely at all of her little jokes.

"Do you know when he'll be back?" I asked.

"Oh, what am I thinking? Of course he's coming back the day after tomorrow. My parents are having their party. You know the one. The big party we have once a year. You guys can come. Why don't you? We'd love to have you."

I wasn't expecting this. "Are you sure your parents won't mind?"

"No, not at all. We get to invite all our friends. Do say you'll come."

She told us when to show up, and we said we would. Then Alex and I said goodbye.

Once we were back on our way down the road Alex said, "Wow! That Clarissa is a peach!"

"She's very cute."

"No, I mean she's really something special. I haven't seen a little fox like that in ages."

"Well, don't get any ideas."

"What do you mean?"

"She's only a child."

"Let's say she's seventeen…"

"More like fifteen."

"But she *looks* seventeen."

"There are laws in this country, you know, concerning minors."

"Yeah, yeah, I know. But I'll tell you, she is really a peach!"

~

WHEN we returned for the party there was a long row of cars clogging the drive and lining the road. We had to park pretty far away. We could hear dance music, and from a distance and with light streaming from its various windows Wetherby regained some of its original magnificence. Once inside, however, one could tell that things were still the same. The house had a dank, musty odor, and in every room, when you looked up, you saw stains on the walls and holes in the ceiling and the molding where the plaster had fallen down. There used to be rats, I remembered, in the old days. There probably still were.

We wended our way through the crowded rooms but didn't see anyone we knew until we came upon Pamela and her high school friends. "Hi," she shouted over the noise. "Charlie's not here yet."

"Where are your parents? I'd like to say hello to them."

"In the kitchen, I think."

Alex had located Clarissa. I couldn't hear what they were saying, but they were smiling and laughing. I took Alex's arm. "Come on," I said very deliberately, "we're going to say hello to our hosts." I practically had to drag him away. I was so angry I could hardly speak. "Just don't—"

"What?" Alex said innocently.

"Don't be an idiot!"

"I'm not."

We found Charlie's mother in the kitchen. She and several other women were busy preparing platters of hors d'oeuvres so we thought we'd better leave them alone. We walked out into the dining room and there found Mr. Morison. He recognized us and gave us a big hello and put his hands on our shoulders. He was a very nice man. "Gee," he said, "I don't know where that son of mine is. He's never been one to be right on time, but he did say he'd make it."

Mrs. Morison came in and spread some trays around the huge dining room table.

"Oh, this will be a treat," Mr. Morison said.

Partly from principle, and partly for reasons of economy, the Morisons rarely ate meat. Thus the trays held various combinations of vegetables on crackers, vegetables cooked in pastry puffs, vegetable pâtés, vegetables fried and poached and broiled and crudité. Such fare was not to Alex's taste. He circled the table twice looking confused and then said, "Jesus! Can we boil the cat?"

"They don't eat meat."

"Well I can see that, you bonehead."

We got a couple of drinks instead and looked around at the crowd. There were Pamela's high school friends, and then friends of Mr. and Mrs. Morison, mostly old country people like themselves along with a smattering of professors from the nearby college. There was no one our age. Mr. Morison must have sensed that we felt stranded. He left the room and came back with a tall, elegant black man, very dark, very powerfully built. He introduced him as Abraham, a friend of Charlie's.

Abraham looked at us both directly, smiled, and said, "You are friends of Charlie's?"

"Yes."

"How do you know him?"

"We went to school together," I said.

"How long have you known him?"

"About ten years."

"I see." He spoke with an accent I could not identify. Since he didn't seem to mind direct questioning, I asked him where he was from.

"I am from Côte d'Ivoire. The Ivory Coast. I am lawyer. International law. I work in city doing law."

I asked him how he came to find himself in this part of the world. At the same time I was trying to keep an eye on Alex, who was looking around for Clarissa.

"I went to Texas," he said. "University of Texas. Austin. Very fine law school. You know it?"

"Oh yes," I said.

"I left my wife and little daughter in Côte d'Ivoire. Then they came to Texas, and I moved here, and they are still in Texas." He shrugged his shoulders and smiled.

"You work in the city?"

"Yes, the city. Very big law firm."

"That must be interesting."

"Very interesting. Very interesting. It is the greatest thing in the world. The law, it is the greatest thing in the world." He smiled broadly. "The law," he continued, "the law, it has no facts. You understand? It is tradition. I say to you that when I practice law I am making law. It is not the same thing when I am done with it. You understand?"

"I think so."

"It is a philosophical problem."

"Yes."

"You agree?"

"Yes."

Alex was slipping away.

"I practice international law. That has special problems. Every society has different traditions, different beliefs of what is true and what is fair. In my country, you see, people do not understand rights. They do not go to law because they do not believe that they have the right to go to law. But here is different. Here people know to stand up for rights. There is no work in my country, but here there is very much work." He smiled again.

"Yes," I said, "we understand our rights here."

"You agree?"

"Yes."

"There is no place for lawyers in my country. They have tradition, but only tradition. The people do not want something new."

"Can they learn?"

"No, no, they are square people. Very square. Square, you call them? Very old fashioned. They do not want to learn."

Abraham led me into another room and told me about his years as a law student. "I would like to do it again. I would do sport penology. Very big money."

"What?"

"Sport penology."

"You can specialize in that?"

"Yes, yes. Very big field."

"I've never even heard of it."

"You will. You will. Sportsmen are the fastest growing group of violent criminals. Communities wish to be advised when sportsmen move into their neighborhood. Much work to be done."

"I doubt if you could pass a law like that," I said.

"You may be surprised."

I looked around for Alex. I was beginning to worry. Abraham sensed that my attention was wandering.

"You know, you would make a good lawyer," he said. "Have you ever thought of becoming a lawyer?"

"Not really."

"You should, you know. You have a good mind for law. You think like a lawyer. I can tell. It is not too late. You are young man. You start now, you will be lawyer in three years."

"Oh, I think I've done all of the studying I'm going to do for a while."

He began pressing the matter, making the same point

over and over, and I was getting a little embarrassed. "I'll think about it," I said. I looked around the room. I thought I should try to find Alex and Charlie. I finally made my excuses to Abraham and shook his hand.

"You will think about what I said?"

"Yes," I said, "I will."

"You will?"

"Yes."

"It will take only three years."

"I know."

"You will be good lawyer."

"I know."

"You will let me know what you do?"

"Yes," I said.

I began to wander through the rooms but without any luck. Finally I got myself another drink and stood on one side of the large drawing room and watched people come and go. After a good twenty minutes, I spotted Charlie passing by in the entrance hall and I hurried over to meet him. He looked the same as always. Tattered t-shirt, blue jeans, a confused mass of blond hair hanging down to his shoulders and over his face.

"Charlie," I said.

"Hey, man!"

"How are you?"

"Great, man! How you been?" I could see right away he was thoroughly drunk, which was not unusual.

"Fine," I said. "We met Pamela the other day and she told us you'd be here."

Charlie looked behind me, then around the room. He seemed confused.

"Me and Alex."

"Oh, Alex," he said with some relief.

"Pamela tells me you're racing skateboards."

"Yeah, man, it's fucked up! Tried out for this team,

y'know, clocked me at seventy-two miles an hour, and this guy says he'll think about it, you know. I said fuck you, man. Seventy-two miles an hour and you'll think about it? Fuck you, man." He laughed.

I was a bit confused myself now. "But you made the team?"

"Oh yeah."

"It sounds great."

"It's something, man. You gotta try it. You'd kick ass."

For as long as I had known Charlie, he had been trying to get me involved in one dare-devil activity or another. First it was cross-country motorcycle racing. Then rock climbing. Then bungee jumping.

"Listen, Charlie," I said. "I was hoping you could help me with something. I've been trying to find Sophia. Do you know where she might be?"

"Sophia?"

"Yes."

"Oh, man, I don't know. I haven't seen Sophia in a while. I think she works in the city."

I could see this was going to be hopeless.

"Yes," I said, "she definitely works in the city. It's just I haven't been able to get in touch with her. No one has."

"Gee," Charlie said. "I don't know. I only saw her once. We went out drinking with some friend of hers. Cindy or Cynthia or something. Down in the Village."

"Who was she?"

"I dunno. Worked in a gallery or somethin', I think."

"Do you remember which one?"

He concentrated for a moment. I felt sorry for him. Charlie never had a great deal of brain power even in the best of times, and in his present condition this was obviously an effort.

"Cynthia, I think," he said at last.

He hadn't followed me at all.

"Do you remember her last name?" I asked.

"No, man." He laughed.

"Can you tell me what she looked like?"

"Blond hair. I don't really remember. We were pretty drunk."

"Do you remember where she worked?"

"I don't know. Some whacked-out gallery. They had like dead animals all over the place."

It was no use. There was nothing there. I changed the subject.

"I met a friend of yours," I said. "Abraham."

"Abraham!" Charlie laughed.

"He's an interesting guy."

"Yeah."

"He told me all about the law."

"Yeah," Charlie said.

"He's an international lawyer?" I made this sound like a question just to draw Charlie out a bit.

"No," Charlie said.

"Abraham?"

"Yeah."

"He is?"

"No." Charlie laughed.

"He's not?"

"No."

"What do you mean? He told me he was."

"No, man."

"He said he was a lawyer and works in the city."

"No," Charlie said.

"He's not a lawyer?"

"No."

"But he just told me he was."

"No."

This was strange. "Why would he tell me he was if he wasn't?"

"He's just got this thing about law, that's all."
"So he's not a lawyer?"
"No."
I felt like a fool. "So what's he do?"
"Abraham?"
"Yes."
"I dunno. Temps, I think."
"What?"
"Temps. You know. Works in offices and stuff."
"You mean temporary clerical work?"
"Yeah, that's it."
"Maybe he works in a law office now."
"Maybe."
"He tried to turn me into a lawyer," I said.
"Yeah," Charlie said and laughed. "He does that to me all the time."

I really didn't understand it. Why would he tell me such an elaborate lie?

"He told me his wife and daughter are in Texas."

Charlie laughed once more. "No, man, Abraham doesn't have a wife."

"Well," I said, "he really had me going." Charlie and I looked at each other and laughed together. This was actually not an unusual situation when Charlie was involved.

Charlie hadn't yet seen his parents, so I said goodbye and let him go. Before long the party broke up and people started to head to their cars. I made one last sweep of the downstairs rooms, but I couldn't find Alex. Then I thought he might be at the car, but when I walked out he wasn't there either. I decided to wait, but, of course, Alex had the keys so I was reduced to sitting on the bumper. The air was getting cold.

I waited for the better part of an hour. Then I thought of something. I walked back to the house in the moonlight. It was all quiet now. The door was unlocked. I walked in darkness through the downstairs rooms, and then took the main staircase to the second floor. Charlie, when we were younger, used to give me tours of the "state bedrooms"— huge rooms with large tapestry-hung beds that we were told never to sit on or even touch because the textiles were too old and brittle. I slowly swept from one bedroom to the next. The doors to all of them were open, except the last. I put my ear to the door. I could hear Alex, and I presume Clarissa, making love inside. I banged on the door as hard as I could.

"Jesus Christ!" came Alex's voice. "Who's there?"

"It's me," I said. "When you're ready to leave I'll be in the library."

"Jesus Christ!" Alex said. "You scared the shit out of me."

I left them and went downstairs.

My eyes had slowly grown accustomed to the dark, and I enjoyed wandering back downstairs through the expansive rooms and having the whole place to myself. I ended up in the library, and, as luck would have it, shafts of moonlight were falling through the windows, making bright silver patches on the floor. This light, of course, reflected back up through the room, so that I could see the books pretty well although couldn't quite read the lettering on their spines. So I pulled down volumes that looked interesting and brought them into the moonlight for inspection. It was a very old collection. Mostly travels and sermons and bible commentary. Then I hit a large vein of classics. Fine leatherbound books, largely Latin, but some Greek, and most from the eighteenth century. Then I hit some novels. These, too, were all old. Nothing had been added, I guessed, in over half a century. I checked just on the off chance that they might have something by Wolfe or Woolf, but I didn't find anything.

I was getting tired, so I stretched out on a big Chesterfield sofa and tried to sleep. As soon as I was still, I heard the swish and scurrying of little feet. Rats, I thought. Rats eat books. I've seen perfectly semi-circular tooth marks on bindings of old leather volumes. Must have some nutritional value for them. Then I thought, this sofa is leather. Maybe they'll want to eat this. Oh, screw it, I thought. They're not going to bother you.

I was almost asleep, but then the sounds changed again. The wind picked up and the trees outside started to sway and a slight low whistle went through the house. Lord knows there were holes enough. Then there was a sudden splash of rain, no more than ten seconds or so. Then it passed, but the sound of the wind remained. I curled up in the leather sofa and tried to sleep.

I don't remember anything after that except Alex shaking me awake.

"Hey, let's go," he said.

"Who...where's..." I looked around.

"She's gone. She's staying with Pamela."

We left the house and carefully pulled the door shut behind us.

~ *Chapter Five*

WE WALKED BACK to the car in silence. It was getting near sunrise. We got in and didn't look at each other. We were both pretty tired.

"I—"

"Don't," I said.

"I'm not going to talk about it."

"Good."

"Aren't you proud of me?"

"Yes."

Alex started the engine and we drove back to the diner. We found a booth and ordered coffee. It came and we drank in silence.

"Alex," I finally said.

"Yes."

"Are you all right?"

"Yeah, sure. What do you mean?"

"I mean are you in some kind of trouble?"

"No. Why?"

"I just thought you might be. You know if you're in trouble you can always talk to me."

"Yeah, I know," he said. "I appreciate that, buddy. I don't know. I just didn't think things would turn out this way, that's all." He paused.

"How do you mean?"

"I mean I thought we'd drive down to the shore, you know, see Sophia, hang out on the beach and relax and have a good time. I really feel terrible dragging you all over the place like this. I didn't think it would work out this way at all."

"And there's nothing else troubling you?"

"No. I just feel awful. This hasn't been any fun for you."

I could see I wasn't going to get any further in that direction. He was simply going to turn everything back to me.

"You think we still have a chance of finding her?" I said.

"Yeah, sure. We'll find her."

"I saw Charlie. He didn't have much to say."

"Tell me."

I gave him what little information I had. "It doesn't amount to much," I said.

"It's not bad."

"It's not much to go on."

"It's really not so bad," he said. "You leave this to me."

We finished our breakfast, and Alex drove us all the way into the city. We wended our way downtown and found a central area of several blocks densely packed with art galleries. "This looks about right," Alex said. "It's like a puzzle and we can start anywhere."

We parked on a street with a lot of bright banners hanging from the second stories and picked a gallery called Rollenhagen. It was showing the work of Karl-Peter Warnock. We went inside.

The first room was broad and high-ceilinged with a shiny wood floor and high white walls. No art, unless we were missing something. We passed through to a second room. It was not so large and not so bright and not so shiny. Still no art, and no people. We walked around in silence. What did it mean, I wondered. A banner, a sign, and then nothing.

We walked into another room even further back and found a young man wearing tiny round spectacles and sitting behind a huge modern desk.

"Where's the show?" Alex asked.

The young man looked at us as though we were idiots but didn't say anything.

"Isn't it up yet?" Alex persisted.

The young man smiled indulgently and said, "You don't get it?"

"Get what?"

"The installation?"

"I guess not."

"You *really* don't get it?"

"No."

He looked at us as though he were spreading enlightenment to benighted morons. Then he drew himself up a bit, and said, with great significance, "It's the context."

"The context?" Alex repeated.

"The context."

"I'll have to remember that," Alex said.

We turned and took a second look at the room, hoping in some small way to absorb the context. It failed to take effect. The young man waited in suspense, I think because he expected us to leave. He was disappointed. Alex turned back to him and said, "You know, I saw a really great exhibition down here about a year ago. It was a whole room full of dead animals."

The young man looked genuinely pained to have to deal with such impossible cretins. "Are you sure you weren't in the Museum of Natural History?" he said.

"No, it was a gallery. Just like this one. I'm sure of it."

"Well, I'm sorry I can't help you, sir," he said with exaggerated formality. "There's nothing like that now. Perhaps you can find what you are looking for elsewhere."

"Yeah, but where?"

"Across the river, perhaps," he said, giving special emphasis to this expression.

"Thanks," Alex said. We walked back through the empty rooms and onto the street. "I think he was just new and didn't know what he was talking about," Alex said. "People who tell you to go across the river are usually from across the river themselves. Let's try this place."

We walked into a second gallery. This one, too, seemed empty of art and empty of people. But then, once we looked closely, we noticed that someone had left tiny, barely perceptible pencil scratches here and there on the otherwise bare white walls. The entire room was done this way. We circled the exhibition once and then walked up to a young woman behind a desk. She was abnormally emaciated, wore black lipstick, and had a large sequined hatpin stuck into her cheek with the point coming out between her lips. Alex smiled and nodded his head knowingly and said, "It's the context, isn't it?"

"Fuck off," the woman said. She had an art magazine open in front of her and began to stab at the pages with her pen. Alex and I exchanged glances. This isn't going to be easy, I thought. Alex explained what we were looking for. The young woman stabbed again at the pictures in the magazine but didn't say a word. The point of the hatpin twitched between her lips. She seemed to be working herself up into a colossal fit of rage.

Alex raised his hands as if to say "All right!" and we walked back across the room and left.

"This doesn't seem to be working," I said.

"She was a bit odd," Alex conceded.

We walked down about a block or so, then took one of the side streets, and then came back up on the next avenue. We looked into each of the gallery windows. Most of them were completely empty. Some had a few photographs hung on the walls. One had a large pile of dirt in the middle of the floor. "There's a lot of space down here," Alex said. "I wonder if these galleries aren't some kind of real estate scam."

"I don't know," I said. "Could be."

We walked on some more, and then something caught Alex's eye. He stopped to have a closer look. In the window of one of the galleries hung a dried side of beef with a pile of grotesquely twisted dried sausages on the floor.

"This is more like it," Alex said.

We walked inside. There were glass cases filled with dried lamb chops, dried skinned rabbits, dried pigeons, and dried, hacked-up chickens.

"Tremendous!" Alex said out loud.

The gallery owner, a tall, balding old man, looked up from his reading, and then looked down.

"This is really great. I love this," Alex said. "This is the best thing I've seen all day."

The owner seemed moderately pleased. He looked up again. Alex went over to him. "Can you tell me about this?"

"Well," the man said, "what do you want to know?"

"Everything!" Alex said.

"Well, obviously the artist is challenging our conventional notions of durable and consumable goods. You've probably heard of some of his performance pieces, in which he gnaws on household appliances and penetrates his body with vegetables."

"Penetrates?" Alex asked.

"Through the anus."

"Ah, of course," Alex said. He looked at me and nodded his head. "That's a signifier." Then he turned back to the old man and said, "I think I remember seeing an exhibition like this last year."

"No," the old man said, "this is completely new. You've never seen anything like this."

"Oh sure, I've seen this before."

"No, you've never seen anything like this."

"Oh yeah, I've seen this. At another gallery. Last year."

The old man looked annoyed. "Well," he said, "you may be referring to the exhibition at Kreiger Gallery. But it wasn't anything like this. Just dead animals, still in their skins. Fur attached. Pathetically naive. Little more than comfortable, old-fashioned bourgeois art—if you call it art."

"Well, okay," Alex said. "Now that you've explained it I can see the difference. This stuff definitely challenges my bourgeois conventions."

Alex looked at me and smiled. Now that he had got what he wanted, he was going to have a little fun at the old man's expense.

"To tell you the truth," Alex went on, "I don't think I'll ever be the same. Without my bourgeois conventions. I can feel them slipping away like…like dead leaves. Gnawing and penetrating. That's the essential point, don't you think?"

The old man wasn't fooled for a second, and he seemed ready with a come-back.

"Thank you very much," I interrupted. We said goodbye and I pulled Alex to the door.

Once outside Alex said, "You know, you shouldn't have done that."

"What?"

"Cut me off."

"Why?"

"I was just getting interested."

"Really?"

"Yes."

"I'm sorry."

"I could feel myself changing, you know. Shedding my old conventions. Transforming myself inside and out. Now it's gone. I've lost it."

"I'm sorry," I said. "I didn't know you felt that way about art."

"Oh, yes, I do. I always have."

"Well, maybe something at the next gallery will put you back in the mood."

We found Krieger Gallery about a block away. It was, not surprisingly, empty. Alex walked straight to the office in back and spoke to a woman sitting, as expected, behind a little desk.

"Hi," Alex said, "is Cynthia here."

"Cynthia," the woman said. "Cynthia Ferran?"

"Yes."

"No. Cynthia hasn't worked here for ages."

"Where is she now?"

"She's over at the FIA Center."

"Oh, yeah, I knew that!" Alex said. "Sorry."

"That's all right," the woman said.

We left. "Things are looking up," Alex said.

We walked over to the FIA Center. This was a very different sort of place. A large white building with offices and exhibition spaces on several floors. We asked the receptionist to direct us to Cynthia Ferran.

"And this is regarding…?" she said.

"It's personal," Alex said. "We're friends of a friend of hers."

She made a call and then reluctantly let us go.

We walked up two flights of stairs to an office and found a small, plain young woman with a very full head of blond hair. "Are you Cynthia?" Alex asked.

"Yes."

"I'm Alex Jenkins, and this is my friend Tom Jones. We're friends of Sophia Weston."

"Oh, you're friends of Sophia," she said. She looked us over carefully and smiled. Then she said to Alex "Haven't we met before?"

"It's possible," Alex said.

"I'm sure we have—at a party or something?"

"It's possible. Do you know Charlie Morison?"

"Sure, I remember him. You're a friend of Charlie's?"

"Yes, he's a friend of ours. We went to school together."

"Oh!" She kept marveling at Alex. "You're *very* familiar."

"Yes. I don't know. Anyway, we were wondering if you'd seen Sophia. We were trying to get in touch with her and Charlie Morison said you might know where she is."

"Well, sure. I see Sophia all the time. I just sent her an invitation to our opening."

"Is she coming?"

"Well, I don't know. People just show up."

There was a pause for a moment. "We send out an awful lot," she explained.

Miss Ferran kept eyeing Alex. It was apparent she found him a pretty interesting little property. Alex knew just how to press this kind of advantage to its fullest.

"When is the opening?" he asked.

"Tonight."

"Can we have an invitation?"

I was rather startled by this, but I shouldn't have been. Miss Ferran had her desk drawer open in a flash and handed over two sturdy printed cards.

"By the way, Cynthia," Alex said, "if you see Sophia, don't tell her we're coming. We want it to be a surprise."

Oh no, she said, she wouldn't.

When we returned in the evening, the atmosphere had changed. The street was lined with limousines, and fashionably dressed people flocked the sidewalk. The entranceway and the stairs were jammed. We walked in with our invitations in our hands, but there was no one to take them.

We started on the ground floor, and walked into a gallery the size of a gymnasium. We looked around for Sophia, but in all the noise and confusion we couldn't see much. There was something written on the wall about the artist and the installation, but we couldn't get close enough to read it. So far as we could tell, there was nothing else in the room except people—hundreds of them.

We went on to the second floor.

Here there was a smaller gallery, but still large enough to hold several hundred people. The exhibition consisted of about fifty three-by-five-inch photographs stapled directly to the wall. We went up to look. They were all perfectly ordinary snapshots of retail stores, fast food chains, and brand name household products. The same banal images repeated over and over and over. Alex looked at me and shrugged his shoulders.

We tried to see more, but the crowd was too thick, and in fact no one other than ourselves was paying any attention to the photographs at all. We looked around for Sophia, but couldn't see her. We walked over to a placard describing the works.

"*The spontaneous creation of value,*" it read. "*The mundane object of desire. The interface of the popular culture.*"

"What do you think?" Alex said.

"I don't know. What do you think?"

"I think it sucks," he said. "I could do better myself."

"It does look like little more than advertising," I said. "Maybe that's the interface."

"The what?"

"Oh, nothing. It says something about an interface."

"Oh."

We looked out over the crowd. "She's not here," Alex said.

"No."

"Let's try upstairs."

We climbed once more and this time found ourselves in a roof garden. It was a welcome relief from the heat and noise. We were high enough that we could see the river in one direction and some colorfully lit-up skyscrapers in the other.

"I think this is getting us nowhere," I said. "I don't think we're going to find her."

"Oh, come on. Of course we will."

"We can't even find Cynthia, and she works here."

"I'm sure she's here."

We walked across the roof to a second staircase. "Let's try this one," Alex said.

We started down but found our way blocked by a solid mass of very well dressed but by now fairly drunk young men and women. Several of the couples clasped each other and shrieked and laughed. It took us a good ten minutes just to get back to the second floor. We saw a woman wearing a FIA card on her lapel and asked her if she'd seen Cynthia Ferran. She pointed across the room.

We struggled through the crowd and managed to spot

Miss Ferran. She was in conversation with a group of young people who either were artists or wanted people to believe they were.

"Hello," she said. She smiled at Alex. "How do you like the show?"

"It's great," he said.

"Do you get it?"

Once again, that question about "getting it." I used to "get" Giorgione fine. His work was poetic and mysterious and beautiful.

Alex cast an appreciative eye around the room, thought for a minute, and guessed, "It's the interface?"

Miss Ferran smiled delightedly, gave Alex a playful punch in the arm, and said, "You got it!" This was really getting ridiculous.

"Have you seen Sophia?" I said.

"Yes, haven't you?"

"No."

"She was right here a minute ago. She came with Sam."

"Who?"

"Sam. A friend of ours." She saw that we were confused. "She Sam, not he Sam. She's tall, has blond hair."

We looked around the room.

"She's not here now," I said.

"You didn't tell her we were coming, did you?" Alex asked.

"No. You told me not to." Cynthia looked genuinely hurt that Alex could have doubted her loyalty.

"Perhaps we should look for her," I said.

The three of us went down to the first floor, walked outside, looked up and down the street, came back inside, climbed all the way to the roof garden, and then went through all of the rooms once more on our way back down.

"She's not here," I said. "Did she say where she might be going?"

"I don't know. If she's with Sam, they'll probably go to VLT."

"What's that?"

"A club." She gave us the address. When she saw that we intended to leave she appeared crestfallen, most likely at the thought of losing Alex so soon. "If she's not there, there's a party at my place later."

"Where's that?" Alex asked.

She gave us her address also.

VLT was to the east of us, so we started across town. It was fairly late now, and many of the cross streets seemed deserted at first, but soon we passed a drunk lying with his head in the gutter. Soon after that a half dozen homeless people huddling individually in doorways and behind a number of garbage dumpsters. We continued on. The sidewalks were strewn with rags and mattresses and damp, decaying old cardboard boxes. It seemed to be getting worse and worse as we progressed.

"Are you sure this is the right way?" I asked.

Alex assured me that it was. We made one more turn and this time the street seemed to be genuinely deserted. Most of the buildings were derelict. The sidewalk was almost impassable with garbage and debris and the air held a sickening smell.

"This can't be right," I said to Alex.

"The address she gave us should be in the middle of this block," he said. We walked farther on. The stench in the air became more acute, and I could just make out a large pool of vomit shining in the glare of a street lamp.

"I think this is it," Alex said.

"What is?" I asked. There was nothing there but a wall covered with graffiti and a crude metal door, also covered with graffiti and with a heavy chain and padlock hanging from it. Alex pulled the chain—there was no door handle—and the door alternately ground and squealed open.

"Alex, you're kidding," I said. "Sophia wouldn't be in there."

Alex looked inside. There was a dark, damp, filthy corridor only three feet wide and about fifteen feet long. In the faint glare we could see that the floor, walls, and ceiling were all covered with more spray-painted graffiti. Alex started inside. I followed him.

Although I was careful not to get too close to the walls, I could feel the damp through my clothes. The air was rank and unwholesome. I couldn't for the life of me have taken a full breath. When we neared the other end I looked back to the street only to have a sudden moment of horror that this was really some kind of trap, and that the crude metal door would slam shut behind us.

When I turned back around I bumped into Alex. He had stopped at a black, splintered door on the left side of the passageway. He pushed it open and went inside.

We were in a room. There was a dim, bare light bulb suspended from a wire on the ceiling. There was a broken-down sofa against one wall, and cigarette butts and other garbage scattered on the floor. We could hear, coming through a door on the other side of the room, the low throb of some kind of music. Alex crossed the room and pushed open the next door. We could hear the music more clearly now. We passed along another corridor to another door, opened it, and went inside.

We entered what appeared to be a large, old, derelict garage. The place was filled with people, mostly what they used to call punks and skinheads. There were punks spitting on each other. Punks banging their heads against each other. Punks sticking each other with pins. Punks drinking and taking drugs and lying on the floor thrashing and kicking each other. Someone walked past us holding his hand to his head trying to stanch the blood that ran down his face and glistened in the lurid light. Somebody spit directly in Alex's face and as though by reflex Alex punched the boy savagely in the face and sent him sprawling. No one took any notice of this. The boy on the floor crawled away. We stopped and looked around.

Along the opposite wall a crude bar had been set up. As my eyes grew accustomed to the gloom I could see that there were some ordinary-looking types mixed in with the punks and skinheads. Then a sudden movement caught my eye. In the far corner of the room a girl turned away from us who looked, at least from behind, like Sophia. She had the same full dark hair and the same alert, erect carriage. She was standing next to a tall blonde. I tapped Alex and pointed, and just as I did so the two girls disappeared through a door in the corner.

"What?" Alex said.

"I think I saw her."

"Where?"

"She went through that door."

Alex headed off quickly and I followed. The door led to a staircase going down. At the bottom there were corridors leading in three different directions. We couldn't see anyone or hear anything, so we had no clue where to go. We listened for a moment more, heard nothing, and then randomly turned to the right. We walked down a dark passageway with doors on either side. Alex suddenly stopped. We stood still and listened carefully and could just make out the sound of slapping and groaning and sighing coming from behind one of the doors. Alex reached for the doorknob.

"Alex, don't," I whispered.

He opened the door anyway. I didn't look. After a few moments he closed it and said, "She's not there."

We walked on some more. The sounds of human agony and human desire became more pronounced and more strident. I kept thinking to myself, "What am I doing here? What the hell am I doing here?" I told Alex we should go back, but he wouldn't. He had to check every room to the end of the hall, and only then would he turn around.

We went back to the stairway to start again.

"I think we should split up," Alex said. "We can cover more ground that way."

"Where do we meet?" I asked.

Alex thought for a moment. "We'll meet here," he said.

"I don't think that's a good idea."

"Then we'll meet upstairs," he said, "at the bar."

I looked around. "Who'll go which way?"

One passageway led straight on and then bent around to the right so that we couldn't see the end of it. The other led directly to a door.

"Let's see what's here," Alex said. He opened the door slowly and we peered inside. There were naked bodies swarming in heaps on the floor. There were people tied and chained to iron contraptions along the wall. I took a step back.

Alex looked at me. "I'll go this way," he said. "You go the other."

"Meet you at the bar?"

"Yeah, meet you at the bar."

I was in somewhat of a daze. I walked back to the staircase and stood still for a moment to get my bearings. Then I took a deep breath and looked up and started down the corridor in front of me.

I wasn't really expecting to find anything, so it gave me a start when about halfway down the passageway I heard footsteps dashing quickly away along the other length of the corridor. I ran the last few steps to the corner and looked around just in time to catch a glimpse of a foot, I felt almost certain a woman's foot, disappear around another bend about ten yards ahead. I dashed there as fast as I could, but that led to yet another hallway that cut across it so I had to stop and listen to guess which way to go. My heart was beating hard and my body was shaking, so for a moment I couldn't tell if it was my own breathing I was hearing or the sounds of someone else. Then, when I finally calmed down, I didn't think I could really make out any sound at all. I looked down each direction. The floors were wet. It was almost completely dark. There was nothing to go on. I chose the one on the left.

 I started to move on slowly and immediately I knew I had made the right choice. I could hear, just barely, the gentle drip and spat of footsteps over the wet floor. I walked forward about twenty feet. I could feel the water getting deeper, and the air was damp and smelled of urine, as though we were descending into a sewer. Before long it was pitch dark and I couldn't see anything. The water was up to my ankles. I had had enough. I couldn't go on.

 "Sophia," I pronounced into the darkness. "Sophia, is that you?" I listened for an answer. I was certain someone was there, but I got no response. I gave up and walked backwards for a few steps. Now that I was no longer pursuing but retreating a kind of horror came over me. I turned and walked quickly down the corridor to the stairs and then dashed up to the bar. I was trembling and out of breath.

 I won't linger over what happened after that, but suffice it to say that I waited almost an hour next to the bar with my back to the wall but Alex never showed up. I really didn't want to go back downstairs, but I screwed up my courage and made one quick sweep to look for him, although I tried only two of the three main halls. I didn't want to go down that last corridor again.

After that I left and walked all the way over to where we had parked our car, but, to my surprise, it was gone. I walked over to the address Cynthia Ferran had given us, but when I reached it all of the lights were out and Alex's car was nowhere in sight, so I didn't bother to ring her apartment. Then I walked around for a while heading north and trying to decide what to do. Well, I thought, there really was nothing to do. I walked the entire fifty or so blocks to my apartment, let myself in, double-locked the door behind me, and went to sleep in my own bed, as I had not done in a week.

~ *Chapter Six*

I SLEPT UNTIL NOON and woke up surprised to find myself at home. Given the events of the last week, and especially the last night, I might well have felt worn and upset, but in fact I was more or less at ease. I got up only long enough to make some coffee and toast and then climbed back into bed, reached over, drew the curtains aside, and watched the tree limbs sway in the wind. I opened the window. A cool steady breeze blew across the bed.

I ate my breakfast and relaxed and then I rummaged around in a small bookcase looking for something to read. I chose a novel that I had completed several years before, had recently set about to reread, and then had stopped. I propped up some extra pillows and spent a leisurely hour and a half before the telephone rang. I thought it must be Alex.

"Hello, Jones?" the caller said. I couldn't identify the voice at first.

"Yes," I said.

"This is Professor Reich. Did you get my letter?" He sounded angry.

"No. Maybe. I don't know. I haven't checked my mail yet. I've been away."

"I know you have. I've been trying to reach you. You need to come to see me, young man."

"Yes, I know," I said.

"I mean today," he said. His voice was shaking.

"I don't know if it's possible today," I said. I started to make up a series of excuses.

"Don't play games with me, Jones. I've notified the police. I'll have you up on charges. You get your little body down here, now!"

I climbed out of bed, put on some clothes, and went down to the lobby to check my mail. There were the usual bills and advertisements and then two letters from the graduate school. I looked at the postmarks and opened them in order. The first contained my fellowship check. The second contained a hastily typed letter signed by Professor Reich informing me that my fellowship had been revoked, I should not attempt to cash any of my checks, and I should come to see him immediately.

I showered, dressed, tucked the check in my jacket pocket, and walked to the corner to catch a bus. I didn't have the foggiest idea what I would say. Of course I was in the wrong. I could offer to try to recover the books and to pay him whatever they were worth if I could not, but I didn't see what else there would be for us to discuss. I assumed out of hand that I would be—indeed already had been—kicked out of the university.

I was extremely nervous as I walked down the hall towards his office. I slowed down as I approached, stopped at the edge of the open door, and listened. Professor Reich was having a conversation with someone inside. I leaned in to have a look. It was another professor. Professor Reich saw me and said, "Sit down outside." There were chairs to the left of his door. I felt as though I had been sent to the headmaster's office at school, which in a way I suppose I had.

Now that he had me in his sights, he didn't mind keeping me waiting. After a minute or two a class let out somewhere upstairs. People filtered down through the hallway and into the lounge. I stared straight ahead and hoped no one would notice me, but before long I sensed that someone was walking in my direction.

"Hello, Jones. Where have you been? Haven't seen you for a while." It was a young man I had taken some classes with named Jeffrey.

"Yes, I've been away," I said.

"Waiting for Professor Reich?"

"Yes," I said.

"Is he your advisor?"

"No," I said. I wanted to change the subject. "How's your research going?" I asked. I knew he had been writing a paper for a Henry James symposium.

"Very exciting," he said.

"James, isn't it?"

"Yes. That's right. Henry James and tribal bisexuality."

Once again, sex, sex, sex. That's all these people ever thought about. I figured I probably would never be seeing him again, so I didn't bother to be polite. "Do you really think that has anything to do with Henry James?" I asked.

"Oh, yes, James was obsessed with the sexual rituals of the tribe."

"What tribe?"

"Late nineteenth-century Europe, of course."

This was just too much. "Well, I hope it works out for

you," I said rudely. I wanted him to leave, but he didn't pick up on it.

"James was always fetishizing and re-fetishizing the other," he continued, "both in gender and in generational terms. Up until now everyone thought this was just one of his ways of negotiating socially constructed binarisms. But now I have evidence that it actually runs much deeper than that."

"Really?" I said coldly.

"Yes." He looked extraordinarily pleased with himself. "I've been doing some research in animal behavior, and you know, it's just fantastic! I still can't believe it. Did you know that in Central Africa there are entire communities of bisexual and pederastic monkeys?"

"Well," I said, "that's comforting to know."

"It explains a lot," he said.

"Doesn't it?"

"It opens the door to a lot of possibilities."

God, I thought, is this idiot ever going to shut up? The prospect of meeting Professor Reich was almost pleasant by comparison. "And you think Henry James would care about that?"

"Oh yes. I think there is a definite connection."

Fortunately, I didn't have to wait long for relief. The man who had been in conversation with Professor Reich left, and I heard Professor Reich in a commanding tone say, "Jones, come in here!"

I walked in.

"Close the door," he said.

I did.

"Sit down." He indicated a chair. He sat down next to me, crossed his legs, and looked at me hard. "I don't know if you realize," he began, "that you, Jones, are in very deep trouble." He paused for effect. "At first I didn't believe it was you, but I've spoken to other people at the party, so I know it was. What were you thinking, Jones? That's what I would like to know. What, really? Just what was going through that little head of yours?"

I didn't have much to say, but he didn't give me a chance anyway.

"You realize of course that I've spoken to the police and they'll arrest you and press charges as soon as I tell them. Do you have any idea, my young man, what the minimum sentence is? The minimum? Three years—in prison. Didn't you know that? What could you have been thinking? Tell me. I'd really like to know."

Once again, he didn't wait for an answer.

"You may have some idea about what you're going to do, but I'll save you the trouble and tell you what you're going to do. You're going to return what you've stolen and then after you've done that we're going to have a long conversation about your tenure here in the graduate school."

So he was assuming that I was coming back. But that was neither here nor there. The important thing was to get the books.

"Look, Professor Reich," I said, "about the books, I didn't take them, my friend did. Of course it wasn't right but I think I can get them back for you."

Professor Reich looked at me strangely.

"I'm not saying I'm not to blame. It was as much my fault as his. But what I'm trying to tell you is that I don't have the books, I really don't have them, but if you give me a day or two I think I can get them."

Professor Reich stared at me with an outraged look on his face. "What the hell are you talking about?" he finally exploded.

I didn't know what was wrong. "What do you mean?"

"What books?" he said.

"The books my friend took," I said.

Professor Reich looked at me uncomprehendingly at first and then leaned back and smiled as though now he was beginning to understand. "Your friend stole some books?" he said.

"Yes."

"And that's what you think this thing is all about?"

"Yes."

"I see."

Professor Reich paused and then leaned towards me and said very pointedly, "My dear Jones, that friend of yours stole much more than some books. He stole a Watteau drawing that my father gave me that's worth over a quarter of a million dollars."

I think my face fairly dropped. I couldn't believe it. I sat there silently with my head swimming. It was a long time before I could speak. Finally I said simply, "I didn't know." I looked up at Professor Reich and when I caught the expression on his face, I felt he believed me.

"I think you should consider yourself on a leave of absence from the university," Professor Reich said. "I'll give you two days to locate the drawing and those books. What were they, by the way?" he asked.

I told him. He winced.

"Two days," he said. "Then we need to talk."

~

I GOT back to my apartment and called Alex, and then called everyone who knew Alex. I called the hospitals to see if they had admitted anyone matching his description and the police to see if they had arrested him. I came up with nothing. I went around to his apartment and spoke to the doorman, but he said he hadn't seen him. I didn't see how I could possibly track him down in just two days.

Then there was another problem: money. I was virtually broke. I had lost my fellowship, my rent was coming due, and I didn't even have enough money to buy groceries. I could take an overdraft at the bank for five hundred dollars, but that was all. I had no savings.

I went downtown to where we had sold Professor Reich's books and spoke to the woman there about buying them back. She told me the price was three thousand for the Woolf and two thousand five hundred for the Wolfe. Where was I going to get that kind of money? I tried to persuade her to hold them for me but she wouldn't. I think she could tell that something was not right, but she didn't seem to care. She said she would sell the books to whoever came through with the cash.

Back home, I racked my brains for some way to raise the money. I called my father, but he, as usual, said that I had to make my own way in the world and that it was a bad habit to borrow money. I was not surprised. That had always been his line. He was not cheap. It was simply a matter of principle.

Finally, I walked to the bank and took an overdraft of five hundred dollars. Then, back home again, I went through my files. I had an insurance policy and even a very small retirement fund from my two years of part-time teaching. I phoned both companies but they told me it was impossible to borrow against my accounts. I wasn't sure if this was exactly true, so started to badger them a bit. I told them that I'd spoken to my lawyer and he said that they had no right to keep me from my money. I told them I would take them to court. But it didn't work. They knew better.

I looked around my apartment for anything I could sell, but I didn't own much besides books. I gathered up a few of the genuinely valuable ones and brought them to the old man on Madison Avenue. From my manner it was probably pretty obvious that this was a distress sale, but he didn't take advantage of it. He offered me three hundred dollars, which was a fair price. I was sorry to see them go. They were some of my favorite books.

I spent the next day once again trying to reach Alex and trying to think up ways to raise enough money to buy back Professor Reich's books. The only thing I could think of were my insurance and retirement accounts. I called both companies again, but got the same response. I was desperate and became rather nasty on the phone. I'm sure they thought they were dealing with a lunatic.

When the second day came, there was nothing to do but call Professor Reich and give him the bad news. He told me I had to see him in person. I took a bus downtown and met him in his office. Once again, he closed the door.

"I don't know what we're going to do with you, Jones," he began. "I've put a private investigator on the case and he assures me he will get results. He has already learned that we're not the only people looking for that little friend of yours. Evidently he has a penchant for other people's goods. The question is, what will become of you?"

I was sitting in a chair in the middle of the room, and he was standing with his back to the window. He stared down at me. "The truth is," he said, "we had very high hopes for you. Several of my colleagues have said so. And now the only course seems to be to expel you from the university."

He paused and started to pace around the room. "I've been trying to think if there is anything you could do to earn your way back into our good graces." He walked behind me and ran his hand along my shoulder. Then he sat in the chair next to me. "We really do think quite highly of you," he said again. "The question is what can you do to earn back our trust." He put his arm around my shoulder and touched my neck. Oh God, I thought. I looked at him and he looked into my eyes and smiled slightly. "Can you think of anything?" he said. He tightened his hold on my neck, leaned forward abruptly and tried to kiss me on the mouth. Holy Christ! I sprang to my feet. He didn't seem a bit daunted. He smiled confidently and stood up and came towards me. "I do so want to be able to trust you, Jones," he said. "And I want you to trust me." He reached out to grab me and tried to get close enough to kiss me. I held him off.

"Stop it," I hissed. I didn't know what more to say. I stumbled towards the door and he followed me and tried to embrace me again. I warded him off as best I could. For some stupid reason I was afraid to raise my voice and have anyone outside hear us. With my back to the door and trying to fend him off with both hands, I said, "I'll find your stuff. I promise. That's all I can say." I stopped, and for a moment I think we both expected more. But there was nothing more. I slipped through the door and closed it behind me and hurried out of the building without looking back.

~

SO far as I was concerned, Professor Reich and his Watteau drawing could go to hell. I didn't steal it and I didn't know where it was. It was entirely his problem.

The books, however, were a different matter. I had helped to sell them, and I felt it was my responsibility to get them back. I was almost five thousand dollars short, but I thought that if I could put together several hundred dollars as a deposit, even a non-refundable one, then that miserable woman at the bookstore might hold them for me at least for a time. It was worth a try.

Thus, my attention shifted from trying to find Alex, which seemed impossible, to trying to find a job, which seemed only slightly less impossible.

I called some of my friends, but they all gave me the

same answer. I had no useful experience, and they already had hundreds of advanced-degree students lining up to make them coffee and take out the garbage. The prospects looked bleak. I searched through my address book one more time to see if there was anyone I had missed, and then I remembered the most obvious thing: that the graduate school had its own employment center which helps place students in jobs around the university. This meant, of course, going back to campus and possibly running into Professor Reich, which was no small deterrent, but I took a moment to overcome my anxiety and then headed downtown.

I walked into the employment center and talked to the woman in charge. She asked me a lot of questions, consulted a tattered book of job listings, and made a few calls. At one point she put her hand over the phone and asked, "Have you studied cultural criticism?"

"Yes," I replied.

"Yes, he has," she said over the phone. It wasn't true. I hadn't studied it. But I didn't think it would matter. She placed me in a job as assistant to the editor of *By Product*, the cultural studies journal of the Marxist Literary Group. The pay was remarkably high, and they wanted me to start right away.

The office of *By Product* was in the same building as the Literature Department, only downstairs in a back corner. The editor-in-chief turned out to be a young, waif-like graduate student named Ashley Cohen. She was unwilling to explain much of anything, sighed when I asked her what I could do, and finally said, "Well, I guess you can read these." She pointed to a stack of manuscripts on a desk. Then she disappeared into a back room and turned on a television. She was watching a soap opera.

I took a look at the first manuscript. It began:

Eclipse ~ *97*

> In recent years it has become obvious to many theorists that the imbrication of class, status and power, based as it has been on patriarchal premises, has led inevitably to the demand for a meta-narrative of the always already agonistic negotiation inherent in the desiring praxis of any identity-based society. This has produced, in the last few months, a renewed demand among theorists for a reconceptualization of power relations vis-à-vis the longstanding crisis in minoritarian identities. Such a race for theory, as it has been called, and the consanguinous search for an apt meta-narrative which at once is an alternative strategy for but yet not a privileging or legitimizing of the dominant discourse, suggests the direction theorists must take in the search for a pre-discursive foundation for language as well as enabling scholars to understand and articulate the knowledge-base and role-level it plays.

Well, there was a lot to work on here. I picked up a sharpened pencil and in the margin of the page I drew a large bracket that contained the entire paragraph and wrote the word "Simplify?" Then I circled the expression "always already" and wrote in the margin "Meaning?" I underlined the words "praxis," "minoritarian," and "privileging" and wrote "Can you avoid these jargon terms? Couldn't you find some simpler, more direct way of saying what you mean?" I drew a squiggly line under "consanguinous" and wrote "Look this word up." Then I underlined the "for" and "of" constructions and wrote "Avoid two prepositional phrases with one object." Finally, I underlined "knowledge-base" and "role-level" and asked "Do you mean anything more than 'knowledge' and 'role' here?" That hardly addressed all the problems in the piece, but I was trying to be realistic. I thought that the author, whoever it was, would have enough to work on with that. The article was eight pages long. I made similar corrections throughout.

When I finished about an hour later, I brought the article in to Miss Cohen, who was collapsed in an armchair watching a commercial. I held it in front of her and said that I thought there were a few problems she should look at. She squirmed in her seat and looked over the first page. An alarmed expression came over her face. She screamed "What the hell did you do?"

"I made some corrections."

"What for?"

"Because it needed them."

"Do you know who this is?" she said. "This is like a totally important cultural critic. You can't edit her."

"You can't?"

"No."

"Then what do you do?"

"Just write 'Publish' at the top and leave it alone."

"Oh."

As I turned to go she said, "You know, I'm not supposed to have to tell you these things." Then she plopped back down to watch her soap opera.

I erased all of my numerous corrections, wrote "Publish" on the top of the manuscript, and picked up the next essay in the pile. It began:

> Among the truly great theorists who don't often get mentioned at all anywhere anymore is Adrienne Ciscous, whose startlingly original work on commodity fetishism and the mythologization of symbolic capital we ignore at our peril. Her brilliant queer(y)ing of subject-to-subject relations under

late capitalism has convincingly exposed how our previous narratives of the subject-position in society have been over-determined by a multiplicity of non-theoretical factors, making it imperative for us to destabilize the very image-constructions we have heretofore been called upon to uphold.

I got up and brought the article in to Miss Cohen and held it out for her to see. I pointed to the name at the top. "Who's this?" I asked.

"Don't tell me you don't know who she is. She's a way famous critic."

"Oh yes, I remember," I said. "It just slipped my mind." I went back to my desk, wrote "Publish" on the top of the manuscript, and moved on to the next piece. It looked like more of the same. I read until quitting time and then stacked the papers in a neat pile and poked my head into the back room.

"I'll see you tomorrow," I said.

Miss Cohen responded with a barely perceptible "Umm."

At work the next morning there was a fat package in the mail. I opened it and saw that it was filled with articles from authors with names like Shibov and Korvas and Popoiescu. They were written in various eastern European languages. I brought them in to Miss Cohen. It was morning so she was watching cartoons.

"What do we do with these?" I asked.

"Write 'Publish' and send to the translators."

"Which translators?"

"In the files."

I looked around. There was a filing cabinet in the front room.

"You approve them before you've read them?" I asked.

"Yeah."

"Why?"

"Everybody does."

"Why?"

"Road Runner" was just starting up, and I could see that Miss Cohen was annoyed at having her attention distracted.

"Nobody reads anglophone writers anymore," she said.

"They don't?"

She looked at me with distaste. "I thought you said you were in graduate school."

"I was."

"Then how come you don't know this stuff?"

I went back to the front room and rummaged through the filing cabinet. It was in a sorry state, but I managed to find a file on the National Association of Scholarly Translators. There were forms to fill out which took me most of the morning. When I was done, I put everything into a large envelope and decided to mail the package on my way to lunch. I communicated these intentions to Miss Cohen, who answered with a kind of grunt.

When I returned, Miss Cohen was not in, so I went back to the filing cabinet to put things in order. Among the many papers thrown in without having been filed was a thick stack of invoices from the National Association of Scholarly Translators. I sat down to look through them, and inevitably my eyes fell to the figures at the bottom. I couldn't believe it. When Miss Cohen came back, I asked her if she knew how much those translations cost.

"No," she said.

"Three thousand dollars a page."

Miss Cohen's face was the picture of unconcern. "The school pays for it," she said.

"But it's too much."

"They can afford it."

This seemed to me a pretty bad reason. "Yes, but shouldn't we shop around?" I said. "I'm sure we can do better than that."

"Look," she said, "there are books you can read about this stuff. I'm not supposed to teach you everything." She went into the back room and turned on the television.

I filed the invoices and then sat idly at my desk. There was nothing to do. I started pondering why a Marxist organization wouldn't look around for the best price. Then I thought of something. I got up and walked into the back room. Miss Cohen was watching a program called "The Young and the Restless."

"Is that why you charge so much for drinks at the cash bar?"

"What?" she said, suddenly startled into consciousness.

"Is that why you charge so much for drinks, at the conferences, because of Marxism?"

"What? No. Look. It's not my job to teach you these things. If you want information go to the library."

"Just explain it briefly," I said. "I want to know."

She rolled her eyes. "It's called economics. The fewer people who buy, the more they have to pay."

I thought about this for a moment. "So you mean that if I were the only person to go to the bar that day, then the cost of my drink would have to equal the normal revenues for an entire day?"

"Yeah."

"I think that's what I did pay."

"If you're done," she said, "I have a lot of research to do." She plopped down into her seat to watch television. I apologized and left.

I took a book out of the bookshelf and sat and read about Marxism for the rest of the afternoon. When it was time to leave, I went in to say goodbye to Miss Cohen.

"I don't think we're going to be needing you anymore," she said without looking up from the television.

This took me by surprise. "I don't understand. You mean you don't want me back?"

"Yeah."

"Why not?"

"It's not working out," she said. "You don't know cultural criticism."

"So you mean I'm fired?"

"Yeah. I can't really talk about it now. I'm doing research."

I took it that this was her gracious way of telling me to get lost, so I didn't question her anymore and left. She had a point though. I didn't really understand cultural criticism. I guess I shouldn't have lied and said I did in the first place.

I walked home quite dejected, and the more I thought about it the more I realized what a fix I was in. How had all this happened? Only a week before I was an industrious if mildly discontented graduate student. I had the next few years of my life mapped out. Now I might find myself in jail at any moment.

Among the many things on my mind, there was the reality that my rent was due on Friday, which was in two days, and I didn't know how I was going to pay it. I had never been late before with any obligation of that kind. Even with my limited resources, I always made it a point to pay all of my bills on time. Now, I thought, my life is going to be different. And why? I thought, why?

I got home and tried once more to reach Alex. What had happened to him? How could he have left me in such a mess? It was very disturbing. His own life had always been filled with mishaps and problems of his own making. Indeed, the very first time I met him, when we were children, he was fighting, and losing badly, to a group of older boys. But he had always righted himself somehow, and he had always treated me as though I were his one sane, stable friend in the world, a refuge from the anarchy that seemed to consume the rest of his affairs. Perhaps it was for that reason, my sense of having a special status and deserving special treatment, that I never delved too deeply into the real basis of our relationship. I realized now I did not know my friend at all anymore, and perhaps never did.

For the next two days I continued to call anyone I could think of who might know anything about him. I called his parents and his sister. They said they thought he was on vacation. That, at least was what he told them when they had last spoken. I called the woman who takes his calls at work. She sounded indignant and said, "Mr. Jenkins does not work *here* anymore." I asked her if she knew where he did work and she said, "No, I have no idea where Mr. Jenkins is employed," and then she abruptly hung up. I was about to give up when I decided to make one more call to the Westons. I thought I'd ask about Sophia first. Mr. Weston answered the phone.

"Sophia?" he said. "Oh, yeah, Tommy, she's around. Had some kind of mixup at work. Needed to get away for a while. You know that girl works too hard. Always did. She's down at the beach house, opening it up. You should go and see her if you've got the time. She could use a little company."

I told him that was very nice of him. Then I asked him if he had heard anything of Alex.

"Alex? No. Last we heard he was with you."

I didn't know how to handle this. I had promised Mrs. Weston I would have him call her. But I had no plan or strategy now. I told him what I knew.

"Well, I can't help you, Tommy. Have you tried his parents?"

I said yes, I would do that, I'm sure I would find him, and with that I said goodbye.

"Give Sophia a call at the beach house," he said.

"I will," I said, but I didn't think I would.

Friday came and went, and with nowhere to go I stayed in all day Saturday waiting for the fateful knock of the landlord on the door. But it never came. By evening I had relaxed a good deal, ordered in Chinese food, and settled down to do some reading. Then, unexpectedly, at about midnight, far too late for the landlord, someone hit the buzzer at the door. I was quite startled. This didn't sound right at all. "Who is it?" I said. I pressed the Listen button, but all I could hear was the sound of traffic on the street. The buzzer rang again. "Who is it?" I said again. I didn't know what to think, but I was getting pretty scared. I listened some more and could barely make out the sound of someone trying to open the door. "Who is it?" I asked a third time. Finally, someone answered.

"Jones," the voice said. "Jones, is that you?"

"Who's there?" I said.

"Jones, you open this door," the voice demanded.

"Who is it? Who's there?"

"It's Reich. Who the hell do you think it is?"

"What do you want?" I said.

"Need to talk to you. Big trouble, you little shit. Open this door!" He started to bang violently on the door. The landlord lived in the basement apartment. I really didn't need this kind of trouble right now. He started banging more loudly. "Let me in!" he shouted. Christ, I thought. He's going to wake the whole building.

I hit the buzzer and let him in. I looked through the peephole in the door and watched him as he staggered into the lobby. I could see him about to knock on the door of the downstairs apartment. I quickly opened my door. "Up here," I said.

He looked around and started to climb the stairs. He was breathing heavily and looked a mess. He pushed past me into my apartment. I could see he was two-thirds drunk. He stood unsteadily in the middle of the room and looked around. "Little shit-hole," he said. I didn't know if he was referring to me or the apartment.

"What do you want?" I said.

He turned and walked towards me. "Big trouble, you. Cops on your ass. Lock you up." He snorted a few low laughs. "Know what to do with the likes of you." He grabbed me and held me against the wall. He was a big man, and even in his present state he was remarkably strong. He started kissing me on the face. I tried to get away but he grabbed my shoulders and slammed me hard against the wall and started running his hands over my chest and around my buttocks. "Know what to do with the likes of you," he said again. I tried as hard as I could to push him away, but he was leaning heavily against me. Now he ran his hand through my crotch and grabbed me hard and started to slide me along the wall towards the sofa

"Knock it off!" I said. I tried to wrestle free, but I couldn't. He was kissing me on the neck and I managed to get one arm free and I punched him in the face as hard as I could. It didn't seem to have any effect. I wanted to cry. I punched him again and again, but he didn't feel a thing. He was holding me bent halfway over the side of the sofa and was trying to work his hand into the front of my pants. Oh, god, I thought, he's going to rape me. He pushed against me harder and we fell over the arm of the sofa and spilled onto the floor. For a moment, he lost his hold on me, and I stood up and frantically looked around. I had a tennis racket in the corner of the room and I ran to pick it up. Reich was on his feet staggering towards me. I don't know what possessed me, but I swung at him with all of my might and caught him squarely on the side of the head. Finally, he stopped, stunned by the blow. And now I must say that rage took over from any instinct of self preservation. I slammed him over again and again on the head with the edge of the racket. Blood streamed down from his forehead. He fell to one knee. I think I would have killed him had he not slowly raised his arm in a movement that was almost hieratic and waved it slowly, dismissively from side to side. I stopped. He turned around, still on his knees, and at first crawled and then slowly staggered to his feet towards the door. He stopped briefly when he'd reached it and held onto the door knob and tried to catch his breath. There was blood on his face and hands which he seemed to notice now for the first time. "Get you, you little shit," he said through his panting. "Send your sorry ass to prison. Know what to do with you. Just wait, you little shit. Just wait." He straightened up a bit and tried the door. I thought he would never get it open, but I didn't have the nerve to step forward and open it for him. Finally he did open it and walked out and then turned and leaned against the doorframe. "I'll get you," he said. "No more fucking around with the likes of you." He turned away and slammed the door. I ran and locked it and stared through the peephole until he was gone.

~ *Chapter Seven*

I DIDN'T SLEEP at all that night, and towards morning I heard voices at the door. I walked quietly to the peephole and saw the landlord speaking to two policemen. I almost dropped from fright. I didn't know what to do; I only knew that I had to leave. I ran around my apartment thinking what I could grab, but I didn't see anything I really needed. I patted my back pocket to make sure I had my wallet, and then I opened the rear window and stepped out onto the fire escape. I could hear voices and the sound of footsteps coming up the stairs. I closed the window behind me as gently as I could. My hands were trembling as I pushed down the fire escape, and I was in such a panic I could barely place my feet on the rungs. At first I tried not to make any noise, but the ladder was shaking and rattling and I knew it was hopeless to try to control it. My feet hit the ground and I scooted out the side alley, which unfortunately led back to the street where the police must have been parked. I turned left on the sidewalk and didn't look back and tried as hard as I could to stride calmly to the end of the block. I turned left once more, still without looking back, but it took all of my resolution to do so because I was really quite scared. The backs of my legs were quivering, telling me to run, but I knew that would be a mistake. I was in agony.

I turned left again at the next block and walked on and on across town. My rational sense told me that they probably couldn't catch me. The city was too big and they had too many more important, more dangerous people to track down. But my emotions told me to run and run and never stop running. So walking fast and steadily was a good compromise. I walked all the way over to Fifth Avenue and then turned south. I didn't have the slightest idea where I would go, but I thought I should get out of the city.

As I got closer to midtown, I debated going to Grand Central and taking a train, but I had no idea where. I could go to Charlie Morison's, but somehow I didn't feel that was right. I could see Richard Atlee, who had his own farm, but I didn't really want to see him any more than Alex did. Atlee was a schoolboy acquaintance who had become intolerable as an adult. It was hard to say why. It was simply the case. Then I thought of Sophia. That had been the original plan: to see her at her shore place. I felt it was a mistake and an importunity before, but now I was desperate. Besides, her father suggested I go. So I wouldn't be showing up completely uninvited.

I walked past Grand Central and started to make my way across town to the Port Authority. I would need to catch a bus to get to Sophia's. It was early morning. Midtown was mostly empty. But as I got closer to the bus station, more and more people appeared on the streets. Homeless men and women sat on the sidewalks against the buildings. Several of them held out their hands and asked for money.

There were groups of men at the street corners who stood in my way and stared at me as I passed. Out of the corner of my eye I caught someone hurrying up to my side. It was a young man in ragged clothes. I moved away from him but he skipped energetically along side of me. "Hashish," he said in a soft hiss. I ignored him. Now he was practically jumping into my path. "Hashish," he said again.

"I don't want any," I said.

"Hashish," he said again. "C'mon, man, I know you get off. What's your trip, man? I know you get off. I got everything man. Smack, coke, crack. C'mon, man. Rich white boy. I know you get off. Just say the word, man. Just say the word."

"I don't want anything," I said. "I don't get high. I'm not cool."

This last statement caught him by surprise. I doubt if anyone had ever said that to him before. He slowed down and dropped behind with a face that showed just the glimmering of a new conception. But it didn't last. He was back at my side in a few strides.

"C'mon, man. I know you're cool. I know you get off," he said, but with somewhat less conviction.

"I told you I don't want anything. Now leave me alone." I picked up my stride, and he let me pull away. I looked back once and he had turned and was walking in the other direction.

I had only one block to go, and I tried to move with some purpose. There were even more homeless people about, some sitting quietly, some begging for cash, some deep into the litter baskets. Two men across the street were yelling at each other and trying, feebly, to fight. I reached the last corner and crossed the street to the station. There was a good deal of activity now. Early commuters were bustling in and out of the building.

I pushed open one of the front doors and someone close to me said softly but distinctly, "Bastard!" Against my better judgment, I turned to look. It was an old bum. To everyone who came through the doors he pronounced, indiscriminately, "Whore! Bastard! Bastard! Whore! Whore!" Well, who knows, I thought. Maybe he's right. It reminded me of a friend in college who used to say, "The world is divided into two groups. Those who call you darling, and those who call you asshole." That pretty much sums it up for most of us, I guess.

I walked through the main hall to the ticket counters and waited in a short but excruciatingly slow-moving line. I hadn't had any breakfast and the adrenalin that had fueled my walk must have finally spent itself. I felt light-headed and thought for while that I might fall over. I had to squat down and put my head between my knees. It was pretty embarrassing. Even in that environment, people were staring.

The woman at the window told me that the bus I wanted, an express, had left a half an hour ago. She said this in an accusing tone as though something had gone terribly wrong and it was entirely my fault. I guessed that this was some kind of defensive strategy she had developed on the job to protect herself from all the stupid people who would yell at her as though it were her fault that the busses left on time. I tried to assure her that it didn't matter to me which bus I took, so long as I could find any bus that would take me where I wanted to go. She sold me a ticket for a local that left at 12:20.

I was hungry but the stores in the station looked filthy, so I walked out of the building to find a decent coffee shop. Most of the ones in the immediate area were also a mess, so I decided to head back across town to see what I could find.

I passed a long block of X-rated video parlors and peepshows. There were a surprising number of people coming in and out. On the next block I started into one coffee shop but the grease on the floor and the stench of cheap oil in the air drove me out. I passed two more shops until I found one that looked possible, but when I took a seat at the counter I could see that it was none too clean either. I didn't care. I needed something to eat. I ordered coffee, eggs and bacon and toast and then immediately thought it was a mistake. The coffee was gray and thin and came topped with a skin of what appeared to be oil and dishwater. I watched the waitress as she flirted with the cook, scratched her armpit, bundled up a filthy plastic garbage bag, placed it in a trash can out back, and returned without washing her hands. She brought me my meal. There was a shiny black hair caught in the grease of the eggs. I felt as though I were going to throw up. I wanted to at least drink a glass of water, but even that looked cloudy. I ate my toast, which seemed all right, and that gave me the courage to try the bacon. Then I put some money on the counter and left.

I walked a little farther east until I found a doughnut shop and had two plain doughnuts and some decent coffee. On my way back I was accosted by a small black woman wearing blue jeans and a t-shirt that she must have slept in for a month. She was completely covered with grease and soot. Her hair was a tangled mess, and she dragged her feet as though she were asleep. "Hey," she said, in a barely perceptible voice, "Hey, you wan' som' ass?"

"No," I said. I walked on faster. She didn't try to follow. I looked back and saw her standing there stranded in the middle of the sidewalk without the slightest idea where she should go or what she should do. "You don' wan' som' ass?" she called after me in puzzled tones.

I got back to the station, but I still had a long time to wait for the bus. More of the shops were open, and I stood at a newsstand and read a magazine. I looked for a place to sit down, but there wasn't any, so I leaned against a railing and watched the commuters and the local inhabitants come and go. It was not an inspiring prospect.

Some policemen walked by, and although I knew it was silly to think they would be on the lookout for me, still it made me uncomfortable. My mind went back to the events of the night before. What confused me most was not so much that someone I had once respected had tried to take advantage of me—indeed had tried to rape me. What disturbed me was that I believed I had genuinely wanted to kill him when I had the chance. It was as though some primal rage and loathing had been welling up inside me and, once it was let loose, it was impossible to stop. I thought of the blood on his face and hands and the strange but positive thrill that the sight had triggered in me. I started to feel ill again.

I walked around looking for the bathrooms. They were downstairs. Inside, the floors were wet and covered with spots of what I hoped was mud. Most of the toilets were splashed with urine. I found one stall that was reasonably clean and wiped the toilet seat with a paper towel. I gingerly sat down but I was there only a moment when I noticed that someone had cut a ragged hole of about four inches diameter in the partition wall. I was looking at the black, hairy knees of the person sitting in the next stall. I tried to ignore it. Then I started again. At first I couldn't identify what was happening. What? I thought. What? There was a black, chapped finger reaching through the hole and wiggling around. What the hell, I thought. I got up as fast as I could and hurried out of the bathroom. What the hell is the matter with everyone? Is this what it is all about? Is this what it comes down to? Everybody settling into their own level of prostitution? I couldn't believe it.

It was still a few hours until my bus left, but I climbed the stairs to the gate and waited by an open end of the garage that looked out over the river. At least I could get some air. Huge busses swept by and their drivers looked at me as though I wasn't supposed to be where I was, but I didn't care. I stayed and watched the boats on the river and looked out over the hills in the distance and the skies beyond.

I went back to the gate when the bus was due, but it didn't come. A number of people were waiting, but no one said anything. They stood there numbly and sullenly. After half an hour I walked downstairs to see if I could get any information. No one knew anything. I was afraid the bus might come and go while I was away, so I hurried back upstairs, but I needn't have. The bus didn't come for another hour and a half. The driver gave no explanation, and none of the passengers bothered to ask.

The ride, once under way, was interminable. In addition to traffic delays, the driver made an incredible number of stops at obscure destinations and then followed a bizarre course back to the main roads. No sooner did I feel that we were comfortably back on track than we would leave the highway once more and crawl along the back roads to another out-of-the-way town.

What would have been a two-hour drive by car stretched into four and five hours. I tried to sleep, for I was nearly exhausted, but I couldn't. It was getting towards evening when we finally ascended the causeway over the bay. The bus driver stopped at a small cluster of shops at the base of the bridge and the last few passengers got out. I waited for him to start up the shore towards the next town, but he didn't. "End of the line," he said. "Everybody out."

I reminded him where I was going.

"That's here," he said.

"No, it's not."

"End of the line," he said again. "Get out."

I knew what he wanted. He wanted to turn around at

the circle and go directly home over the bridge. If he took me to where Sophia lived that would be five miles out of his way and then another mile or so beyond that before he could turn the bus around and head back. I didn't argue with him. There was no way I could win, and I was too tired anyway. I wanted to tell him he was a lazy bastard, but I didn't have the energy, or the courage, to do that.

I stood on the street and tried to get some feeling back in my legs. I had a long walk ahead of me, but I looked and felt a wreck and didn't really want to show up at Sophia's in that condition. I knew a diner about a quarter of a mile in the opposite direction so I headed for it. The sun was getting low in the sky.

Once at the diner I went straight to the men's room and splashed some water on my face. My neck felt grimy so I undid my shirt and washed my neck and shoulders. My hair was a mess and I wet my comb and ran it through my hair several times. It didn't help much.

I sat at the counter and drank coffee and ate a grilled cheese sandwich. I was terribly thirsty and drank about four glasses of water. I looked out the window. It was getting dark now. I went to the phone and tried to reach Sophia, but there was no answer. Oh well. I'd come all this way, and I wasn't turning back. I left the restaurant and started the long walk in the dark.

The night was fairly clear and there was a light, cool breeze. I could hear the sound of the surf beyond the dunes. There wasn't much traffic. Occasionally I was caught in the glare of headlights of a car coming towards me, or I would see my shadow thrown out in front of me by a car coming behind. Other than that, it was a quiet walk. My body warmed up from the exercise, and there was something comforting about those moments in the pitch black when everything was quiet except for the sound of my own breathing and the surf in the distance and the crunch of my steps on the road.

Most of the shore places were still closed, but here and there I saw lights and caught glimpses at odd angles of rooms, picture-hung walls and shadows moving across them. Then there was a long stretch of dark. I could see Sophia's house a good way off. A light was on.

I started growing nervous again and slowed my pace as I got nearer. My eyes focused tighter and tighter on that lighted window. I thought I saw a dim shadow pass along a wall. I came to within about fifty feet of the house and stopped completely. I was in the middle of the street and I moved over to some bushes by the side of the road. All kinds of strange emotions passed through me. I felt almost as though I had come home. No, that's not right, I thought to myself. It's not your home, and never was. But it felt like it was, or that it should be. What if things could go back to the way they once had been, I wondered—a time that now was almost a dream, but a dream that I might one day re-enter, that might, mysteriously, take me into its heart and hold me just as Sophia had once taken me into her arms, and held me, and, then just as mysteriously, had cast me out. A shadow passed along the wall. I was trembling. I wanted to be there, inside, but I was afraid that if I took even one more step some spell would be broken and the longings that had been reawakened in my breast would vanish forever. The shadow passed again. This was getting serious. I had to do something, but I could not determine what. I imagined the sound of a doorbell at night in a lonely house. I thought of the glare of the outdoor lights that would certainly be turned on. I wasn't ready for that. I needed a moment longer in the dark.

The shadow passed once more. I thought of something. Slowly, silently, I pressed my way through the bushes that protected the back yard. I stood silently inside. I saw that the light was coming from Sophia's bedroom. I crept towards it, my vision narrowed to a slit, alert to the slightest movement. I reached the wall of the house beside the window. My heart was pounding. I felt the veins in my neck throbbing and a pain in my throat as though I couldn't breathe. I tried to compose myself. A shadow flickered against the far wall. As slowly as I could, I slid sideways and got my eyes level with the bottom of the window. I looked inside.

At first, I couldn't tell what I was seeing. Somebody was naked. It was Sophia. She was kneeling with her head thrown back and her mouth open and her eyes closed. Then I saw with a shock that there were two people. Arms and legs. My knees went slack. Sophia was moving slowly up and down, shoulders hunched over now with her hair falling before her. A man underneath her ran his hand over her sides and over her breasts and then around her neck and pulled her down. She held his face in her hands and kissed him several times. I saw that it was Alex.

I turned away and this time did happen to fall and banged against the wall of the house with my head and elbow, making a loud thump. I thought of holding still for a moment but then panicked and ran. I ran through the bushes on the other side of the yard and over the dunes and towards the beach. I didn't stop running until I had to because of the sea. It took a long time for me to understand what I had seen. I was a bit deranged. I walked back and forth along the beach talking to myself, but I couldn't say anything more than "I can't believe it!" over and over again. I started towards the house and then realized that was impossible and then started down the beach and realized that was futile and turned around again. I could have been stuck like that till eternity.

Slowly, after what felt like several hours but was not that long, the frenzy wore off, I calmed down, and my feelings resolved into a dull and constant pain about my breast. I was exhausted and dizzy and thought I would collapse. I looked around me. No spot on the beach looked any better than any other. I fell down and curled up and held myself for warmth. It had turned into a cold night.

When I woke in the morning it was damp and I was stiff. I got up and shook myself and looked around. There was a jogger far down the beach running away from me. I remembered where I was and why I was there. I walked slowly to the house and rang the doorbell. Alex answered it. He seemed perfectly normal.

"Hey!" he said, "How're you doing?"

I stared at him. I was so hurt and confused I didn't know what to say. There was a long pause. We started to speak at the same time.

"I saw you."

"How are—"

"Last night. I saw you."

"What—"

"With Sophia."

He looked at me with some alarm, looked back into the house, and then said, "We have to talk." He led me to the end of the porch and sat behind a wicker table. He motioned me to sit opposite, but I stood.

"When did it start?" I said.

"What?"

"Between you and Sophia."

"Look, I know what you're thinking—"

"When did it start?"

"I don't know."

"What do you mean you don't know? When?"

"Look, kid, I can explain everything. Just sit down."

"Tell me!" I said.

There was a long pause. At last Alex said, "I've always been with Sophia."

"What do you mean?"

"I mean I've always been with her."

"You mean you went out with her?"

"No. I didn't really go out with her. I've just always seen her."

"Even when she was going with me?"

"No, not when she was going with you."

"Before?"

"Well, yeah. Before—and after."

"You never told me." I looked down at my hands. They were trembling. I couldn't believe this was happening. How could he have deceived me in this way? "You told me she wanted to see me," I said.

"She does."

"How can you say that?" I snapped.

"She does."

"You just spent the night with her."

"Look, kid," Alex said, "you just never got it. Sophia would've slept with you."

What was the matter with him? Was he insane? "What are you talking about?" I said.

"You can sleep with her right now, if that's what you want."

"God! What the hell's the matter with you?" I could have hit him I was so angry. Alex was taken aback, but only for a moment.

"Look, somebody had to tell you. That's just the way it is. Sophia'll sleep with anybody. That's just the way it is. I'm sorry."

"Shut up."

"It's true."

"I don't believe it."

"I know you don't, but it's true. She's slept with me, she's slept with Morison, she's slept with Atlee—"

"I don't want to hear this."

"—Kirk, Bob Gould, that black guy who hangs around with Morison—"

"Enough."

"—Kenny Everett—"

"Enough!" I said.

"To tell you the truth, I think you're about the only guy we know who hasn't slept with her."

"Shut up. You're so full of shit. I don't believe any of it."

"I wanted to tell you, I really did, but you had her built up into some kind of goddess."

I stared out at some distant clouds. I didn't believe a word of what he was saying. It didn't sound like Sophia.

"What you do is your business," I said, "but you shouldn't have led me on."

"I didn't."

"How can you say that?"

"I didn't. Look—"

"Why did you want to bring me here last week? Why did you say that Sophia wanted to see me?"

"Because she does. She really said those things. She thinks you're the greatest. She thinks you're the nicest guy she's ever met."

"Oh, shut up," I said. "Just shut up."

"It's the truth."

He wasn't making any sense. "You know how I feel about her," I said. "And still you slept with her?"

"Sleeping with Sophia's no big deal."

I got up. "I'm not listening to this." I started to walk towards the beach. Alex said something but I didn't catch it. I was too angry and didn't want to talk to him anymore.

I sat on the sand and looked out over the ocean and tried to calm down and think things through. I'd never been so mixed up in all my life. How had all of this happened to me? What had I done to deserve it? Sophia wasn't the problem. If she wanted to be with Alex that was her business. But why would my oldest and best friend abuse me in such a way? I couldn't understand it.

I tried to consider what I should do next. I didn't see many alternatives. I had no money, no home, no job, and now, it seemed, no friends. I was feeling pretty sorry and miserable for myself.

I heard the sound of someone walking over the dunes. I turned and looked. It was Alex. I turned back and looked out over the ocean. Alex sat down a dozen yards away from me. It took a long time before he could say anything. Finally he said, "Look, kid, I'm sorry. I'm really sorry. You're right. I've been a complete jerk. I know I have. I want to make it up to you. Really. I want to make it up to you."

"I don't see how you can," I said.

"I was desperate, all right? I was in a really tight spot. I wasn't using my head. God, I'm stupid!" He slapped himself on the forehead. What a faker he was.

"Knock it off," I said. I didn't want to make it easy for him.

"Look," Alex said, "I'm going to tell you the truth. The whole truth. All of it. You can have me put in jail if you want, but here it is."

"Go on."

"Well, Sophia and I, you know, we used to have lunch together a lot, and one day she happened to mention how they handle securities at her shop, I mean bearer bonds and government bonds and things like that. Well, I couldn't believe it, you know. It didn't sound possible. I mean, they didn't log them in right at all. So there was a period, oh, of about forty-eight hours or so, when those bonds just didn't really belong to anybody, you know?"

"So?"

"Well—"

"So you took them."

"Sure."

"What's that got to do with me?"

"I'm getting to that. Everything looked all right, and then all of a sudden Sophia disappeared. She just vanished. I couldn't find her anywhere. She had the bonds. They were worth a shitload of money. So I thought maybe she'd run out on me. Then I thought maybe they caught her and they cut her a deal. You know, screw the other guy and we'll go easy on you."

I still didn't get it.

"Look, I was in a tight spot. If she was working with them then I couldn't call, because they'd nail me. But if she was double-crossing me, and taking everything for herself, then she wouldn't talk to me anyway. You see? Either way, I couldn't get at her."

"So you needed someone who could."

"Yeah."

"And that was me."

"Yeah. I knew she would talk to you. She's crazy about you."

I thought about this for a moment. "But she's with you now," I said.

"Yeah. She was just spooked, that's all."

"You found her at that club?"

"Yeah."

I didn't want to think about it. Sophia at that club. "Is she in trouble?" I said.

"No. We sold everything. There's no evidence. Nobody can prove a thing."

"It's as simple as that?" I said.

"Well, we don't have them. They can't prove we ever did. And even if we did, they can't arrest us for stealing something they never really owned in the first place."

He seemed to have an answer for everything. "So what do you do now? Go off to Tahiti for the rest of your lives?"

"No. Probably go back to stockbrokering."

I really thought he had lost his mind. "How can you? You're a crook."

"Not proven."

"But everybody knows it."

"First, they don't. Second, they don't give a shit. It's ancient history. I start with a new firm, produce, get results, nobody cares."

"And that's it?"

"Sure."

"Everything's fine?"

"Sure."

"And you don't care about your reputation? About honesty, loyalty?"

"You're sounding like your old man now."

"My father told me a businessman can never tell a lie."

"Well, kid, I hate to tell you this, but it's just not like that anymore."

"I guess it's not."

"Today," he said, "people only want you for what they can get out of you."

For the first time, I looked at him directly. "You ought to know," I said. I hit my mark with that one.

"Look, Jones," Alex said. "I didn't mean to get you mixed up in this. I really didn't. I thought—I was hoping—that this business with Sophia would turn out all right and then the three of us would relax here and have a good time."

"With you and Sophia?"

"No, with you and Sophia."

"You're despicable," I said. I don't think he understood what I meant.

"Look. I said I want to make it up to you, and I mean it. I'm gonna give you forty thousand dollars. Cash."

"Oh, come on. That's not the point."

"Fifty?"

"That's not the point. I don't want your money. It's just… Listen," I said, "We were friends. I trusted you. I never thought you could treat me this way."

"Look," Alex said. He got up and walked over and sat down next to me and tried to put his hand on my shoulder. I shrugged him off. "Look," he said again, "we are friends. We are. We've always been friends. But I know you. I've known you, what? All your life."

"All your life. I'm older."

"Right. That's why I'm telling you this. You just never got it. You never did. You were always different from everybody else. You were. You were like from a different planet. Sophia was crazy about you, man. She was always crazy about you. You just didn't pick up on it."

"I don't know what you're talking about," I said.

"Well, you know, kid," Alex said, "you can't just sit around holding hands with a girl all the time."

I stood up and turned towards the house. I didn't want to hear any more. I'd had enough. I started to walk back over the beach towards the road. Then I thought of something. I stopped on the top of the dunes and called back to Alex, "You stole a drawing."

"What?"

"From Professor Reich. You stole a drawing."

"Oh, that."

"Yes, that. You'll get arrested for that."

"No, I won't."

"It's worth a quarter of a million dollars."

"Oh, bullshit. It is not."

"It is."

"Is that what that butt-man told you?"

"Yes."

"Well, he's full of it. I only got two thousand. I sold it to the guy who bought the bonds. He can kiss that baby goodbye."

I walked past the house and I started down the drive. Alex followed me.

"What are you doing?" Alex said.

"I don't know."

"Let me give you some money."

"No," I said.

I turned and walked out the drive and onto the road.

"Look," Alex called, "let me know if you need anything."

I didn't answer him and I didn't look back. I felt my affairs with him were at an end. That was it. I picked up my pace down the road.

I had no idea where I would go or what I would do, but at that moment I didn't care. It was early morning and the road was deserted. There were low dark clouds over the bay and it looked as though we might get some rain. I set my eyes into the distance. I shook out my head and arms and took a few deep breaths. It was going to be a long walk.

~ *Chapter Eight*

IT HAS BEEN over two years since that day. I had vowed never to speak to Alex again, but of course things didn't work out like that. He called me so frequently and apologized so slavishly that after a while I felt it was silly not to talk to him. So we thrashed it all out and now he is officially forgiven, although I don't see him often and I'm always a bit wary when he calls.

Just as Alex had predicted, he and Sophia soon found new jobs with different firms. Within a few months, he said, no one could even recall what the whole fuss was about. I asked him if he had ever heard anything more from Professor Reich, but all he said was "Who?"

Sophia I ran into once in the subway. She spotted me through a gate near the token booth and called my name. Instinctively we both reached out and so found ourselves awkwardly holding fingertips through the metal bars. Immediately she was embarrassed and let go. We spoke only for a moment. I asked her if she was going my way but she said she wasn't. I've never seen her since.

As for myself, I landed a job with the state government as a kind of glorified messenger boy. The secretaries like me because, they tell me, I'm the only one who comes back. The other messengers disappear for the day after they finish their first delivery.

When I'm not busy carrying messages, I'm put on loan to one of the state archivists. I work in the basement sorting through the files of dead and long-forgotten legislators. It's moderately interesting. The archivist gives me a list of criteria for what documents to preserve and what to throw out. Most of what I read gets thrown out.

About a month ago I was visiting my family in the country when I ran into Charlie Morison. He was in a bar, alone, drinking. He was happy to see me. I asked him how his skateboarding was going but he told me he was out of that now. His new thing, as I understood it, had something to do with jumping out of an airplane with a kind of surfboard attached to one's feet. He said it was "the greatest free fall in the world" and that I should give it a try. I told him I didn't think so.

Charlie had gone out with Sophia for over a year, so he knew her well. I asked him if he thought Sophia had always gone around with Alex, and he said yes, she always had. He was surprised that I didn't know. Then I asked him if he thought Sophia had had affairs with any of our other friends. He said he didn't know, but he didn't think so. And Abraham? Charlie just laughed. No, he said, Abraham doesn't like women. "He prefers men?" I asked. No, it's not that, Charlie said, he just doesn't like women.

Then Charlie told me that his father had finally decided to sell the mansion and all the property. The state was planning to buy it and turn it into a park. I had thought that of all of his family Charlie would have been the last to be upset by such a thing, but I was wrong. Growing up at Wetherby meant a lot to him, and he was extremely depressed.

I don't own a car, so when I left Charlie I walked down the hill to the station and caught a train to take me back to the city. The track winds along the Hudson, and normally I find a seat on the river side because the sunsets are so beautiful over the mountains. This time, I didn't. The sun had set on a lot of things that had once been bright. I didn't want to see any more.